P.S. NEVER IN A MILLION YEARS

J. S. COOPER

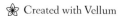

For my Great Aunt Lilian Enid Waldron,
November 1923- January 2022
I will miss you!

BLURB

To My New Boss

You are an asshole. Maybe I'd even call you a boss hole. We've never even officially met because you're worried all of your lower assistants will "fall for you and make a pass." You sent your executive assistant to give me a list of "to-do's" that were so basic I thought I was in preschool. And let's not talk about your "never-do's." You can only wish I would make a pass. You would be so lucky as to even catch a glimpse of my fine ass. In fact, why don't you kiss it instead? Jerk.

Also, I'm not taking a vocabulary or algebra test. Just because you're the CEO doesn't give you the right to be pompous and arrogant. And frankly, I saw that photo of you in the newspaper last year; are you cousins with the yeti? Not a good look.

You can keep your $25 an hour. My self-respect is worth more than that. And no, I'm not interested in any of your other offers.

Marcia "I have self-respect" Lucas

P.S. Never in a Million Years

I'm not crazy—I never intended to actually send the email. It was just a draft email I wrote to vent. I needed the paycheck way too much to go off on my boss. Only when I went into the office the next day, there was a note on my desk. It read, "Got your email. A million years is up. See me in my office. Your boss, Finn 'The Yeti' Winchester."

My dad was right: my mouth would eventually get me into trouble. Only he had no idea just how bad the trouble was going to be.

ONE

"I got the job. I got the job!" I sang to the beat of "I Saw The Sign" as I ran into my tenth-floor studio apartment looking for my best friend, Susie. She was sitting on the worn tan leather couch that we'd found outside a brownstone in the West Village, chewing on a black pen and staring at some papers on her lap.

"What are you doing?" I headed over to the couch, pausing to admire the Persian-looking rug I'd picked up at a flea market a few weekends previously. The reds stood out against the dark wood floor. And even though the fabric was ratty, it was better than the deep scratches in the wood that the previous renter's illegal tiger had created. I had a feeling I already knew what Susie was studying so intently, and I didn't really want to hear the answer. I was the sort of person that liked to live in La-La Land for as long as possible.

She looked up at me with a furrowed brow and made a face. Her lips were stained black by the pen, indicating to me that she'd been working on our finances for at least a couple of hours. "I'm trying to figure out how much money we need to pay off our bills this month." Her light brown eyes were filled with worry.

My heart started to pound uncomfortably. That expression meant things were not looking good. Which I'd already known, but I preferred to forget that our bank account contained less money than the piggy bank of Jason Lowenstein, a five-year-old I'd babysat on the Upper East Side just the week before.

"Oh, we'll figure it out," I said, trying to stay upbeat. "Don't worry about it, Susie. Didn't you just hear me? I got the job. We're in the money!" I danced around the room, twirling like I was still in second-grade ballet class. "Today is a good day. I also won $20 on the scratch-off as well." I didn't tell her that I'd spent $40 before finally scratching off the winning ticket.

"Oh, congratulations. Marcia. That is absolutely amazing." Susie dropped the pen and papers on the couch and jumped up to give me a hug. "So how much are you getting paid, and... Okay, well, let me just back up a little bit. Which job did you get? Not the executive job?" There was disbelief in her voice, which offended me a little, but she was right to be skeptical.

"Well, I got *a* job." Just because I'd gone in for an executive job didn't detract from the job I'd actually gotten. A job was a job. And who cared about small things like job titles?

"What do you mean you got *a* job?" Susie's smile dropped from her face faster than a groupie's panties drop for Adam Levine. "Please don't tell me you're going to be working as a secretary for Mr. Singh on the fifth floor. We both know his 'Adopt a pet chicken as an emotional support animal campaign' is not going anywhere."

"Poor Mr. Singh would be devastated to know you think so little of his latest idea." I held my head up high and sniffed at her. I imagined that's how members of the royal family gazed at commoners who deigned to say something rude to them. "But anyway, no, I'm not working for Mr. Singh... again. I mean, I didn't get the job I applied for, but I got a job."

"So, tell me more about this job." Susie pressed her lips together. I knew that she was being patient with me. Neither one of us had expected me to get the actual job I'd applied for, though I'd secretly hoped for a miracle. There were stranger things than me getting a job I had zero qualifications for. Shit, half the actors I saw on TV couldn't act to save their lives. They were truly just getting by on their looks. Just once, I'd like to get by on my looks as well. It wasn't like I'd applied to be the president of the United States.

"So, as you know, I submitted my application to become president of marketing at Winchester Enterprises."

"Yeah, girl. I'm not sure what you were thinking."

I shrugged. We both knew I had zero qualifications to become the head of marketing. I'd never marketed anything before in my life, aside from myself on dating apps, and that hadn't worked out very well. I was a whiz at making myself look better in Instagram photos, but that was all thanks to an app on my phone.

"I was thinking that God would hear my prayers, and they would be open to on-the-job training," I giggled. "But anyways, I didn't get that job, even though it would've been amazing because it paid $250,000 and we both know how far that much money would go."

"Marcia, you don't even have any experience with marketing," Susie pointed out. You probably would have been sued by Winchester Enterprises for a refund of your salary."

"That's not exactly accurate. I mean, I'm on social media all the time." I grinned. "But fine. Yeah. They said the same thing to me, you don't have the requisite qualifications, blah, blah... but it turns out they were looking for a bunch of temps, so..." I flossed from side to side. "Your girl has sold out to the corporate giants."

Susie's face fell. "You got a job as a temp? Doesn't that mean you won't have the job forever?"

"Well, yeah. I mean, that's part of the name. Temporary. But if I do well, I can stay, and they're looking for more people, so I think you can get a job there too."

"I don't know." She pouted. "I was really hoping to try and get a job as a substitute teacher."

"Girl, you do not want a job as a substitute teacher. Plus this job is paying $25 an hour. If we're both making $25 an hour, that's $50 an hour."

"True."

"And we'll be able to pay off everything really soon if we're making that kind of money. What do we owe right now, anyway?"

"We owe electricity. We owe water. We owe gas. We owe two months' rent, also cable and internet. I think they're going to turn it off soon."

"No, they can't turn off the cable and the internet! How are we going to watch our shows?"

"Do you honestly think the cable company cares, Marcia?"

"Well, perhaps if I call them and..."

"Call them and what?"

"Say that you moved out."

"Then they'll just turn the service off." Susie was fast losing patience with me.

"But then I could reopen the service in a new name!"

"Isn't that illegal, Marcia?"

"Hey, I'm not Marcia. I'm Anne." I grinned at her. "Anne Baxter." I changed my voice. "Hello, I'm Countess Anne Baxter of Chickentopia, and I would like to establish service at my new residence."

"Oh my gosh. No." Susie giggled and shook her head. "You cannot do that again. Girl, they threatened to call the cops on you for impersonation last time."

"What last time? You mean when I tried to get the free pizza? That was different. We're just trying to get by right now. We're two young, independent single women in the city, and we haven't quite found our groove yet."

Susie grimaced. "Yeah. You can say that again. Sometimes I think we'd be better going back to Florida."

I put my hand up in a *stop* gesture. "No! We are not going back to Florida."

"Yeah, but we could live at home—"

"Girl, we're twenty-five. Do we want to live at home?"

"No, but at least there was a swimming pool and—"

"And your mom and dad's rules, and I know that my mom and dad also had crazy rules and no, no, no, no, *no*!" I was almost screaming now. "If we give up now, we're never going to make it, and we'll end up marrying two bozos and living in the sticks."

"I don't know about the sticks." Susie looked put out. "Orlando's not exactly the sticks."

"Drive thirty minutes in any direction, and where are you?"

"Fine. We'll stay here, but you need to start bringing in some money—"

"I will have a paycheck at the end of the week because I start tomorrow, and guess what?"

"What?" she said through narrowed eyes.

"We get paid every week."

"Okay, well that does sound good."

"And if you come with me tomorrow morning, I bet I can get you a job as well."

"Hmm, I'd rather you ask them first before I come. What exactly is the job?"

"To be honest, I don't really know. They said they needed a little bit of this and a little bit of that."

"Oh my God, Marcia. What does that mean?"

"I guess it means they'll need a little bit of this and a little bit of that." I had been thinking about which handbag I'd use on my first day when the supervisor had talked about the duties. I mean, it wasn't like they wouldn't tell me again.

"But what's a little bit of this and a little bit of that?"

"I don't know. Receptionist, secretary, PA, EA, whatever. I'll do it."

Susie sighed. "Why do I have a feeling this job is not going to last long?"

"Trust me. I'm a good worker."

"No, you're not."

"Yes, I am."

"Marcia, you hate working. You said you wanted to get married to a billionaire and live a life of luxury."

"Yeah, well I haven't met any billionaires, or even millionaires, and I'm not exactly living a life of luxury." I looked around our cramped studio apartment. "I mean, come on now. We barely have space to throw a rat in here."

"Do not even tempt fate. You know, I heard something the other night."

"It was probably our neighbors."

"In our apartment, in the corner, chewing on my shoe?"

"What? It was just a friend coming to say hello. Maybe it was Ratatouille."

"You know you're a fool." She was trying to look mad but she giggled anyway.

"I know, but shall we go out tonight to celebrate?"

"Celebrate what?"

"My new job, of course."

"Girl it's not like..." She paused and sighed. "Fine. We'll go out tonight and celebrate, but we're not spending a whole bunch of money. We can get one drink each."

I rolled my eyes. "I feel like you're my husband."

"I'm a woman."

"Well, then I feel like you're my wife."

"We're not lesbians."

"You know what I mean."

"I do," she grinned. "But until we've paid up all our bills, we can't afford to spend a lot of money."

"But we have credit cards."

"And we also have credit card bill payments."

I groaned. "Oh my gosh. I love you, Susie. You're my best friend, but sometimes..."

"Sometimes what?"

"You annoy me."

"Why? Because I'm trying to keep you out of the poor house?"

"Girl, look where we live," I giggled. "We're already in the poor house."

"Yeah, and we need to save so that we can get to the rich house."

"Yeah, that would be nice. I mean maybe we..."

"Don't even say we're going to get there on our temp salaries, girl. We're not going to be making enough money to move into a two-bedroom apartment off of Central Park making $25 an hour."

"Well, maybe if I get that president job."

"You're not getting that president job," she giggled. "You don't even have the qualifications."

"What? I have a bachelor's degree."

"In art history."

"So. Maybe I'll become president of a museum."

She rolled her eyes. "Sometimes..."

"What?" I said innocently.

"Nothing." She gave me another quick hug. "I'm proud of you, though. I'm glad you got a job."

"Me too. We really do need the income," I admitted. "And who knows? Maybe they'll see my skills and realize that I could be president." I paused. "Okay, or if not president, I'll get a permanent job. Maybe something that pays a little bit better."

"That would be cool. And yeah, I'll come by tomorrow afternoon, if they say it's okay. It does pay more than substitute teaching, and I guess I won't have to be around little kids."

"Because you know little kids annoy you."

"I didn't say they *annoy* me. I just—"

"Girl, you lasted one month as a nanny."

"Fine. They annoy me," she laughed. "Okay. Shall we get ready?"

"Sounds good."

We both walked to our small sections of the room and started to change. I smiled as Susie put on some music. I loved living with my best friend, and I loved that we were so close. I never wanted that to change—even though I did want our apartment to quadruple in size.

TWO

"So, Susie, tonight we shall party. Let's paint the town red."
I grabbed my best friend's hands and spun her around in
glee. No one paid any attention to us. There was always a
weirdo doing or saying something in the streets in New
York City. I started dancing, feeling happy. "Let's pop
bottles in the sky and..." I sang along to a made-up beat.

"Wow, Marcia..." Susie looked like she wanted to laugh.
"I said we could have one drink. We're not going to be
popping any bottles of anything. You just got a job as a
temp. I mean, I'm happy you did," she added quickly when
I pulled a sad face, "but we still need to save as much money
as possible."

"I know, but a couple of drinks won't break the bank.
Come on, Susie!" I spied the bar on the corner, The Owl
and the Pussycat. There was an illustrated sign of an owl
and pussycat in a boat at sea under a crescent moon. "Let's
dance the night away and have some fun. I know you've
been the caretaker of our finances since we got to New
York, but we're on the right track now."

"Okay, fine." She looked down at her black dress. "I guess I didn't get dressed up for nothing."

"Exactly, chica. We're hot. We deserve to have some fun." I grabbed her hands again. "We're living our dream, Susie. Granted, we're not where we want to be yet, but we can see the light." I grabbed the lipstick from my handbag and reapplied it. "How do I look?"

"Beautiful as always." Susie smiled at me warmly. Her light brown eyes surveyed my face and she gave me a thumbs up.

Susie's long black hair hung in curls down her back. She was a little skinnier now than when we'd arrived, and I knew it was due to stress. We'd moved to New York together, and we'd underestimated how easy it would be to get good-paying jobs. I also knew this had been more my dream than hers. She'd come with me because I'd begged her to, but I knew she would be just as happy in Florida. Sometimes I felt guilty about everything, but I couldn't have survived without her.

"Come on, doll." I pulled her towards the bar. "Let me get you drunk."

We made our way through the double doors at the entrance into a packed and noisy bar. The air stank of stale beer, and there were stickers all over the walls. It was a true dive bar, and I loved it. I pushed past a group of guys who were ogling us, angling towards an open spot I saw near the bar.

"Come on. There's an open space at the front!" I hurried over to grab it before someone else did. I tried to signal to the barman but he was ignoring me. "I guess it will be a few minutes before we get a drink."

"Looks like it," she nodded. "But I need the restroom.

I'll be right back." She looked around and made a face. "Hopefully I can find it. It's packed in here."

"Good luck." I laughed as she walked away. It was then that I became aware that there was a man standing next to me. I looked up and tried not to ogle him. He had to have been at least six-two with a muscular body that told me he worked out far more than I did. He had deep green, sparkling eyes, and dark brown hair. The intense way he was looking at me made me feel a little overwhelmed. I looked away because I was horrible at flirting, but I could still feel his gaze on me. I took a deep breath and decided to be as flirtatious as I could. What did I have to lose?

"Hi," I said, smiling up at him. "See something you like?" *GROAN, that was awful.*

"I don't really know how to take that comment." He looked me up and down. "Why? Do you see something you like?"

"Yes," I said, and he gave me a self-assured grin. I could tell from the look on his face that he knew just how handsome he was, and I couldn't stand cocky men. I pointed at the bottles behind the bar. "Lots and lots of alcohol."

"Touché," he said, laughing. "Nice to meet you." I caught his gaze resting on the top of my breasts before he looked back into my eyes.

"I wouldn't say we've met yet, so I don't really know that you can say it's nice to meet me," I pointed out. He chuckled as I looked him over from head to foot. Definitely too handsome for his own good. And mine.

"I noticed you and your sister coming into the bar—"

"She's not my sister, she's my friend." Many people assumed Susie and I were sisters as we both had black hair and brown eyes.

"You're both very beautiful." He grabbed his beer and took a sip. "But you seem particularly fiery."

"Sorry, not tonight."

I knew men like him. Men who complimented you and made you feel like a million dollars. Men who took you back to their apartments and fucked you with their tongues like it was their job. Men who made you orgasm before they even entered you. Men that made you scream out. Men who were gone before breakfast.

Men that made you cry.

As much as I wanted a night of passion, I wasn't ready for my newest mistake. No matter how much his emerald eyes dazzled me with their keen and focused stare, I didn't need to be the center of his attention tonight.

"Not tonight what?" He raised an eyebrow. "Can I not be a gentleman?"

"We both know what you want." I pressed my lips together.

"What I want?" He shook his head. "You're the one that asked me if I saw something I liked?"

"That wasn't an invitation into my bed."

"It doesn't have to be in a bed." He licked his lips slowly and I swallowed hard. This man was trouble. And I knew trouble all too well. My middle name was trouble. And broke. And heartbroken. I didn't need any more trouble in my life.

"I'm going to have to say not tonight, not ever, no thank you." I turned away from him and tapped my foot in beat to ACDC's "You Shook Me All Night Long." I sang quietly along to the lyrics as I waited impatiently for Susie to make it back.

"I haven't yet, but I could." The whisper in my ear made me jump.

"Sorry, what?" I glared at the man I'd been talking to.

"I can have your earth quaking, though." His lips twitched. He was teasing me.

I was about to respond when I felt a tap on my shoulder. I turned to see Susie.

"Back." She grinned. "Man, this place is packed. Did you get our drinks yet?"

"No, not yet. What do you want to drink?"

"I could buy you ladies your first drink," the man next to me said. I wasn't sure why he wasn't getting the hint. Just because he was a hottie he thought he could get any woman he wanted.

"No, thank you." I rolled my eyes. "I can buy a drink for myself and my friend."

"I didn't think you couldn't, but—"

"Look, dude, my best friend and I are here celebrating, okay?"

"That's nice—"

"And so I'm not going to sleep with you or do anything with you, so you can back off."

"Okay, then. I didn't expect that you—"

"Whatever." I put my hand up and turned back to Susie. "So, did I tell you that the CEO of Winchester Enterprises is worth $10 billion?"

"Winchester Enterprises?" The man cleared his throat and tried to talk to me again. I looked at him.

"Stop eavesdropping on our conversation, but yes, I work there."

"You do?" He stared at me for a few seconds, his eyes narrowing. "In what capacity?"

"She's just a—" Susie started.

"I'm actually one of the presidents of the company." I gave him my best contemptuous look. I had acted in a lot of plays in high school and knew how to look snooty. This man needed to be put in his place. He might be hot, but I was rich. Well, in my dreams.

"You're a *president* at Winchester Enterprises?" He tilted his head to the side and sort of squinted like he was trying to place me.

"Yes, I am actually the head of marketing."

Susie was staring at me, wide-eyed. I hoped she didn't blurt out the truth and make me look like a fool.

"You're the head of marketing at Winchester Enterprises?" The man stared at me for a few seconds. "Wow. I'm impressed."

"Yes. So now you know why I don't need you to buy me a drink, thank you very much."

"Well, maybe I should be asking you to buy me a drink," he chuckled.

"Why?"

"Because you must make so much money working for... What's the CEO's name again?"

"Mr. Winchester," I said, not even blinking. "And sorry, I don't buy drinks for broke-asses." *Pot meet kettle*, my inner voice was mocking me.

"Oh, so you're not on a first-name basis with him, then?"

"Well, I mean, he's Finn to his friends like *me*, but you're not his friend."

"No, I'm not his *friend*." He shook his head. "But I've heard of him. Read about him in the papers."

"Yes. Well, he's in the papers a lot because he is a billionaire," I said. "But excuse me, like I said before, I'm having a private conversation with my friend, and I don't want to be rude."

"No need to be sorry for calling me a broke-ass and

being rude." His lips twitched again. "Go ahead with your conversation with your friend."

"So," I said to Susie. "I was looking..." I paused and looked over at the man. He smiled at me in that devastatingly bone-tingling way that men who are too handsome for their own good do. His green eyes seemed far too knowing and seductive. I wanted to kiss him, slap him, and run away all at the same time. "We can talk about it later," I said to Susie. "Know what you want to drink?"

"Yes. Let's get some margaritas. I feel like some tequila."

"Sounds good. Strawberry?"

"Yes." She grinned. "Should I go and look for a table?"

"That would be great. Are you hungry?"

She paused. "Well, I'm kind of, but..."

"It's fine. I got this." I gave her a meaningful look. If she brought up the fact that we didn't have money to pay our bills in front of this guy next to me, I would scream.

"Okay. Just some mozzarella sticks or something, okay, Marcia?"

"I'll see what they have. Now go and find a table." I watched as Susie hurried and then I turned back around.

"The nachos are really good," the man next to me said. I wasn't sure what his problem was or why he thought I was interested in chatting with him.

"Okay."

"And so are the chicken wings."

"Okay."

"If you and your friend are hungry, I would definitely recommend them. The onion rings are good, too."

"We're not going to eat all that. And I'm not going to get any onion rings tonight."

"Oh?" He raised an eyebrow.

"No. If I'm going to be making out with a hotty tonight,

I don't want onion breath." I looked at him poignantly. "And when I say a hotty, don't get your hopes up."

"I am not getting my hopes up." He shook his head. "But are you trying to say you don't think I'm hot?"

I stared into his gorgeous green eyes and at his handsome face, and I didn't know what it was about the smile on his face that made me want to lie, but I just wanted to bring him down a peg or two.

"You're not my type. I mean, I'm sure you're someone's type somewhere." I shrugged carelessly.

I didn't know why I was being a bitch. Well, that wasn't true. I was being a bitch for all the women like me who'd been dissed by all the good-looking men like him, men who always thought they could get whoever they wanted. And I wanted him to know that he couldn't get me, not in a million years. Maybe it was because I'd been burned in my last relationship, but I was over good-looking guys, especially ridiculously good-looking guys, which this man was.

"Okay. Well, I guess there's a first time for everything." He took a sip of his beer.

"What's that supposed to mean?"

"I mean, you're the first woman who's ever said I'm not attractive."

"Oh, well," I shrugged. "I guess there's definitely going to be more of that coming."

"Okay." He drained the last of his beer. "Well, I guess I will bid you adieu and go and find someone else who's interested in talking to me."

"I guess you should do that."

"Yes, I think I will. So anyway, good luck at Winchester Enterprises."

"Why would I need good luck?"

"I mean, as the president of marketing I would assume

that you have a lot of pressure on you. I've heard that Finn Winchester is a very demanding boss."

"He's actually quite wonderful," I said. "He loves me. He treats me like a daughter."

"He treats you like a daughter?" He raised an eyebrow at me. "How old are you?"

"Excuse me?"

"I'm just saying you look young, but not that young. How old was Finn when he had you? Ten?"

"Obviously, he's not my actual father." I lifted my nose up in the air and stared at him through narrowed eyes. "I'm just generalizing our relationship and stating it is akin to family."

"*Sure.*" He laughed.

"What's that supposed to mean?" I glared at him.

"Nothing," he said, shaking his head. "Well, good luck with everything."

"I don't need it. Bye," I said, waving at him.

He gave me one last stare that I couldn't quite interpret and then walked away. I let out a huge breath as the bartender came to take my order. I didn't know what had come over me, but just the way he'd been looking me up and down and the tone of his voice—absolutely everything about him had rubbed me the wrong way. And maybe I shouldn't have lied, but who was he to know that I wasn't really the president of marketing and that I was a lowly temp? I mean, unless he was a temp at Winchester Enterprises as well, he'd never know.

I ordered the drinks and some mozzarella sticks and then looked around to see where Susie was. I hurried over, grateful that she found a little corner spot, and slid into the seat next to her. "Oh my gosh, that guy was so annoying."

"I didn't think he was so bad," she said. "He was actually really cute—"

"Ugh, I don't even want to talk about guys right now. Let's just talk about my new job and all the awesome things we're going to do with all the money that I make."

"Well, you're not making that much, Marcia. And don't forget, you've got to try and get me a temp job too."

"Trust me. It's in the bag. They're going to love me. Who knows? Maybe if I pray on it and manifest it, I'll become VP of marketing."

"Girl," Susie shook her head and sighed, "you've got about as much chance of becoming VP of marketing as I have of becoming president of the United States."

We looked at each other and burst out laughing. She was right, of course. There was no way that I would ever be the VP of Marketing at Winchester Enterprises. Not unless hell froze over.

THREE

"Okay. Don't look, but that guy from the bar is staring at you," Susie leaned towards me as we sat and munched on our greasy mozzarella sticks.

"Which guy?" I said, turning immediately to look at the bar.

"I told you, don't look!" she hissed.

I immediately regretted looking. It was the annoying guy again. He obviously saw me looking because he lifted his drink up in a cheers.

"Oh my gosh. What is that guy's problem?" I turned back to Susie without raising my glass back to him.

"I think he likes you."

"Whatever. He is such a player."

"Um, you don't even know him, Marcia. Why do you think he's a player?"

"He's gorgeous, and guys like that are always players."

"You shouldn't judge a book by its cover."

"Really? Who says I'm judging a book by its cover?"

"You think he's hot."

"I never said he's hot."

"Girl, you just said he's gorgeous."

"Okay. Well, maybe he is gorgeous, but that doesn't mean I think he's hot." I sighed and rubbed my forehead. I knew I wasn't making sense. "Girl, you know how it is. Ever since Jeremy..." I sighed.

"I know." She squeezed my hand. "He was a jerk, but not every guy is a jerk."

"Most good-looking guys are, though. They think they run the world."

"That's not true," Susie said, though she sounded kind of half-hearted.

"Yeah, it is."

Jeremy, my ex, was the reason I'd wanted to leave Florida so badly. The fact was I could barely call him a boyfriend. He was a guy I'd met on a dating website who had said he was looking for his "true love." His words about wanting to find his fairytale princess had seemed so romantic that I'd jumped at the chance to meet him. We'd gone on about three dates before he'd kissed me. And he hadn't even tried to get into my pants. He'd been absolutely gorgeous and charming. I'd really thought he was the one.

I'd slept with him on the sixth date. And it had been pretty amazing, I couldn't lie. We'd spent the weekend making love, and I'd never been happier. But then he ghosted me for two weeks. I'd been devastated, but then he'd come back, and he'd said he was a covert spy with the CIA and been on a mission. He hadn't ghosted me on purpose, he said; he just hadn't been able to contact me. And I'd wanted to believe him so badly that I ignored all the holes in his story.

So I'd allowed him to take me on another date to make it up to me. We'd gone drinking and dancing, and he'd flirted with other women and barely paid me any attention. I hadn't wanted to bring it up because I didn't want to argue with him. I'd just been so happy that he'd called me again.

We'd gone back to his place and hooked up again, but the sex had not been as good. There had been no foreplay and he'd basically gotten his and then rolled off me. The worst part had come when ten minutes later he'd yawned and said, "Are you leaving now?"

I'd stared at him, perplexed. "I thought I would spend the night." I tried to cuddle up next to him.

"Oh, I prefer sleeping by myself." He'd rolled over and so I'd slid out of the bed and left in tears.

He'd called me a couple of days after that, asking if I wanted to go out again. And me, like the fool that I was, had said yes. We'd met up for a coffee and he'd slipped his hand under the table and tried to squeeze my leg and touch other parts.

"What are you doing?"

"What do you think?" He'd pushed his finger through a circle he'd made with his thumb. "Want to fuck in the bathroom?"

I'd been shocked. "What is going on here?" Like a dumbass, I still thought he was interested in an actual relationship and not just sex.

"What do you think?" he'd replied.

"I don't know. That's why I'm asking."

"You're a good time girl, Marcia." He'd grinned at me. "I mean, you have to know a hot commodity like me gets around."

He hadn't even noticed the tears welling in my eyes.

I hadn't seen him again after that night, but I'd felt humiliated, heartbroken, and embarrassed for months. The fact that I'd even believed he was with the CIA had told me just how desperate I was. Six months after the end of that relationship, and now here I was with Susie in New York, living my best life. But I was still over really good-looking guys. I wasn't going to give any of them a chance ever again.

"Well, don't look now," Susie said, "but I think Mr. Hottie is heading over to us."

"He better not be heading over to me, or I'll throw my drink in his face."

"You can't afford to throw your drink in his face," Susie said, with a slight giggle.

"I can. I—"

"Excuse me, ma'am," said a deep voice.

I looked up and scowled. "Yes?"

"Marcia?"

"Yeah? What do you want? I think I made it very clear when we were at the bar that I'm not interested. So can you please leave me alone?"

"Well, this is awkward." Based on his self-assured smile, he didn't feel awkward.

"What's awkward?"

He held up his hand with a credit card in it. "You left this with the bartender. I assume that you do want your credit card back, Miss Marcia Lucas? Or did you just want the bartender to keep it? He said you'd closed your tab."

"Oh." My cheeks got hot. "Thanks." I held my hand out. "You didn't have to bring the card over. I would've realized I didn't have it and gone back to the bar," I lied. There's no way I would've remembered that I left my card at the bar until I'd gotten home.

"Well, you're very welcome, Miss Lucas," he smiled. "I mean, being an executive at a company like Winchester Enterprises, I'm sure you must have an extremely high credit line, so I didn't want anyone to have access to your credit card and spend all your money."

"All my money?" Was this man making fun of me?

"Well, you must have a credit line of at least $50,000, right?"

"Well..." I bit my lower lip. My credit line was $1500, but I didn't want him to know that. "I have a credit line of $60,000 actually. What's yours?"

"Oh, it's definitely not $60,000," he said, a smug look on his face. "Well, it was nice seeing you yet again."

"Yeah, I would say likewise, but I don't like to lie." I smiled at him.

"Touché." He nodded politely, smiled at Susie, and then walked away.

"Oh my gosh, Marcia, why were you such a bitch to him?"

"He's a smug, arrogant asshole. He knows I don't have a credit line of $50,000. Let's be real. Who has a credit line of $50,000?"

"Uh, maybe someone that's, say, president at Winchester Enterprises," she giggled. "Didn't you say that they make, like, six figures?"

"Yeah. High six figures as well. Some of them even make seven figures. Why do you think I applied for the job?"

"Oh my God." She giggled. "And you really expected to get it?"

"I mean, what's that saying? You don't win any races you don't bet on."

"I've never heard that saying before," she said. "But anyway, I'm proud that you got a job, even if it's only as a temp."

"Thanks, girl." I lifted up my glass and took a huge sip. "And you never know, maybe one day I will be a president at the company. Maybe."

"Yeah, girl. Maybe one day, pigs will fly."

"What's that supposed to mean?"

"I mean, I'm just saying you have absolutely no background to become a president of Winchester Enterprises. And I've read articles about the CEO, and let's just say—"

"Which CEO? My best friend Finn?" I interrupted her, and we both laughed.

"Yeah. Finn Winchester. And let's just say he doesn't suffer fools gladly. You'd be out on your ear before you could even blink."

"Yeah, well, isn't he out in the country climbing some mountain or something?"

"Oh, is he?"

"Yeah, I think he is in the Himalayas or wherever Mount Everest is."

"How do you know?"

"Because they had an article and a photo of him, one of the only photos that's ever been printed, and he had a thick-ass beard. He looked like a mountain man."

"Oh, really?"

"Yeah. Like some sort of yeti," I giggled. "At least I know I won't be falling in love with my boss."

"Aw, shucks. And here I thought you'd get an in with the boss and get me a job as president, too."

"Oh, Susie, you're too much!"

"I take after you," she said, and we both laughed.

I sat back and took another sip of my drink before slowly looking back towards the bar. The man was staring at me again, and I wondered what he was thinking.

I wouldn't have admitted it to Susie, but a part of me wanted to go up to him and just kiss him. And part of me wanted to go up to him and drag him into the bathroom. He was hot, and there was something about his smugness that turned me on. But that was my problem. I was always attracted to the bad boys, and I needed to stop. I needed a good man in my life now, and I knew that man at the bar was certainly not a good one. He'd be good for one night, but I wasn't looking for one night anymore.

FOUR

"Good morning and welcome to Winchester Enterprises." A friendly woman with hazel eyes and shoulder-length black hair greeted me. She was wearing a silk top and a diamond necklace that made her look far too sophisticated to be a receptionist.

"Good morning..." I paused and looked at her nametag. "...Shantal, I'm here for my first day."

"Ooh, yes?" She leaned forward and smiled at me. "What's the position?"

"Head of..." I stopped and giggled. "I'm just a temp."

"I'm a temp, too. You'll love it here." She looked around. "I've been here for about three months, and it's a really nice environment."

"Well, I'm glad to hear that." I was surprised to hear she was a temp. She seemed so comfortable and at ease.

"Mr. Winchester is all sorts of fine," she continued, lowering her voice. "Not that I would tell him that, of course."

"Of course." I was surprised at how friendly and open she was seeing as this was my first day. I also wondered about her taste. In the photo I'd seen, Finn Winchester had looked as fine as a battered can of paint.

"You can sit over there." She pointed to some chairs in the corner of the lobby. "All the new hires are to wait there until Gloria from HR grabs you." She made a face. "Don't let Gloria get to you, by the way. She thinks she works at the White House and that Mr. Winchester is the president or something."

I smiled. "She takes the job seriously then?"

"You can say that again." Shantal laughed and then her expression changed quickly. "Good morning, Gloria, I was just telling..." She raised an eyebrow as she stared at me.

"Marcia... Marcia Lucas."

"I was just telling Marcia here all about how amazing it is to work at—"

"I see." The older lady frowned at me. She looked down at her clipboard and checked something off with the pen in her hand. "Marcia Lucas, you're here from ABC Temps." She looked me over and frowned some more. "We have you down in an assistant role."

"Sounds good to me." I gave her my most winning smile. Gloria appeared to be in her late sixties and was wearing a flowery top and navy-blue slacks; the outfit didn't scream professional or seem to go with her demeanor. Her hair was in a tight bun, and her light blue eyes were framed by thick heavy glasses.

"Wait here." She marched over to the chairs and spoke to the other women sitting and waiting. I swallowed as I looked over at Shantal, who was smiling at me.

"Don't mind her. She's not that bad. She reminds me of the women in my church back home. She's holier than thou in the office, but she's not so bad after work." She rolled her eyes and shook her head. "On Friday, the church ladies are up to all sorts. And then come Sunday, you would think they were related to Mary, Joseph, and baby Jesus."

I laughed at her little story. Shantal seemed like a hoot, and I was already thinking that we would become work besties—if I could keep the job. "Where are you from?"

"Atlanta," she replied. "Moved to the city about two years ago to make it as a singer. It hasn't worked out yet."

"I'm from Florida." I smiled back. "And I know what you mean. I thought I'd be making indie documentary films by now, but here I am."

"I knew I liked you, Marcia. Have a great first day." She beamed at me and then her phone rang and she picked it up. "Good morning, thank you for calling Winchester Enterprises, how may I direct your call?"

I looked over in time to see Gloria heading toward the back with seven women behind her, all of whom looked as nervous as I felt. I tried to make eye contact with a couple of them, but they all looked away quickly. I glanced back at Shantal, who gave me a thumbs up. I waved then hurried to catch up with the other women.

"Now ladies, I don't have to tell you that we require everyone to be professional," Gloria said as she scribbled something on her pad. "And punctual. There are five ladies who are late, and they will no longer be starting today. Follow me." She turned around and walked down a narrow hallway towards some doors that said EMPLOYEES ONLY.

"Normally you will require a badge to gain access." Gloria stopped next to the doors and surveyed us all. "Those of you who are still employed at Winchester Enterprises by the end of the day will go to security and have badges made."

"Excuse me," I said, clearing my throat and sticking my hand up the way I did in elementary school.

"Yes?" Gloria raised an eyebrow and pressed her lips together. I found it hard to believe that she was any friendlier outside of work hours.

"I have a friend to recommend, and I was..." My voice trailed off as Gloria's expression became downright frosty. I'd have to tell Susie I tried, but it seemed unlikely I could get her a job as well. She'd have to apply via the temp agency as well.

"Winchester Enterprises is a privately run corporation," Gloria continued. "It was started in 1902 by Colton Winchester, the great-grandfather of our current CEO." She paused. "Can anyone name him?"

Of course, I knew his name, but I wasn't about to put my hand up again. A blond bombshell next to me spoke up.

"His name is Finneus Augustus Winchester, but he goes by Finn." She looked very self-assured. Maybe my Google skills weren't as on point as I'd thought, but then I remembered I'd read the one newspaper article with him hiking Mt. Everest and then gotten bored and watched *Emily in Paris* on Netflix. Next time, I'd be more diligent about my research... Not that I even cared what some old-ass CEO looked like. It wasn't like I'd have to be in his presence at all.

"That is correct," Gloria said looking approvingly at the blonde. "You're Lilian. Is that correct?"

"Yes, ma'am," the blonde next to me said with a smile, "I'm hoping to join the accounting team eventually."

"Well, we shall see," Gloria said. "Now we're going to go through. Keep your hands to yourself, your eyes to yourself. We're going to be in training today and there will be several different departments talking to you."

"Um, I have a question," I put my hand up.

"Yes, Ms. Lucas?" Gloria looked disapproving. I had a

bad feeling that she didn't like me, which was unnerving because this was only my first day.

"Um, when I was told I was going to be an assistant, I wasn't exactly sure who I was going to be an assistant to, and I was wondering if I would get that information?"

"Once you go through the individual training modules, then we shall determine who you're best fit for."

"Okay. Do I get a choice...?" I chewed on my lower lip. Maybe I was pushing it a little bit too much.

"No, you don't get to choose."

"I'm hoping to be Mr. Winchester's private PA," a short Asian girl said, and a bunch of the girls laughed.

"Me too," said the blonde next to me.

I looked at them both. "Why? Is he a really good boss or something?"

"Or something," the blonde looked at me like I was crazy.

"None of you," Gloria interrupted us with a cold stare, "will be working directly for Mr. Winchester. You are all temps, and you are all on a ninety-day probation. If you do work that we find to be highly acceptable, then we will think about hiring you full-time. If you don't, you will not last the ninety days. Do I make myself clear?"

"Yes, ma'am," we all said quickly.

"Wow. I didn't realize we were working at the White House," I whispered to the blonde, and she grinned at me.

"You would think so, right, with that bitch."

"Excuse me?" Gloria turned back, pinning her gaze on me. I froze. "What did you just say?"

"Who, me?" I squeaked.

"Yes, you. What did you just say?"

"Um, I just said this makes me think this is what it must be like to work at the White House," I stuttered. Oh my

God. Susie would absolutely kill me if I lost my job on the first day.

Gloria continued staring at me for a few seconds and then her phone rang.

"Saved by the bell," the blonde whispered as Gloria answered it.

"Hello, Mr. Winchester!" Gloria was almost beaming into the phone. I guess even she wasn't immune to the big boss. "I'm with the new hires now. Yes, sir, we're about to go into the training room. Yes, sir, we have eight girls today. Um, I did tell the temp agency that we were looking for men as well. Yes, sir, I will let them know. Yes, sir. Yes, sir." She paused, "Why, thank you, sir. Um, well, we do have several." She paused again, "Okay, sir. We'll test for that. Thank you, sir." She hung up, "That was Mr. Winchester." She was almost beaming with pride as she looked at us, "As it happens, he will be needing another assistant to join his team. So one of you will be lucky enough to work in his offices."

"Oh, my gosh!" squealed a redhead, "Really? No way. Not in Mr. Finn Winchester's offices. Oh my gosh!"

"I wouldn't mind working in his bed." The blonde next to me murmured, and I looked over her as she shrugged, "I mean, we're making what? $25 an hour to do work? I wouldn't mind making $2,500 an hour to be his girlfriend."

"Yeah, right. He's going to pay you to be his girlfriend." I paused and looked at her. "Like, are you serious? Does he actually pay people?"

"You're gullible, aren't you?" She laughed. "He doesn't need to pay people."

"Why? On account of he's so rich?"

"On account of he's so rich and—" she paused as Gloria cleared her throat.

"Enough, ladies. We need to go to the training now. Whoever passes the tests with the highest score will be the new assistant for Mr. Winchester. However, you will still be on probation, and—"

"La-di-da-di-da," the blonde whispered again, giggling.

You're going to get us in trouble," I whispered.

"Yeah, well, who cares?"

"Do not say it again," I said.

"Okay," she grinned, "Also, thanks."

"Oh, why?"

"For not ratting me out. That was cool of you."

"Oh, you're welcome."

"No, that was really cool. You could have lost your job, and—"

"I mean, if I'd thought I was going to lose my job, I would've ratted you out." I grinned.

"Fair enough." She laughed, "I'm Lilian, by the way."

"Lilian, nice to meet you."

"You too. And, well, may the best woman win." She grinned.

We made our way into a large, brightly lit boardroom. I looked around. The table was long and wide, and there were chairs all around it. I grabbed a chair and sat down. There was a folder with a pen on top of it. I looked around the table and counted fifteen folders.

"As you can see, fifteen people were meant to start today." Gloria walked to the front of the room. "Only eight of you have made it this far, so count yourselves lucky. If all eight of you get your name tags today, well then, I guess I haven't done my job."

"What?" Did she want new hires or not?

"I'm here to weed out the best of the applicants, and if you falter in any way, you'll be gone."

"Way to motivate us on the first day," I mumbled.

Gloria fixed her eyes on me. "Excuse me, Ms. Lucas?"

"I said we're all new here. We all came for a job, but you're almost making us not want the job."

"If you don't want the job, you can walk out the door right now."

"Um, I do want the job, but..."

"But?"

At that moment, there was a knock on the door, and a handsome man with blond hair walked in. "Hey, Gloria." He grinned at her and looked around the room. He lifted his hand up and gave a wave, "Hey, everyone, I'm Sebastian. Nice to meet you all."

"Hi," we all chorused.

I studied Sebastian. He was very handsome, but not so handsome as to be an asshole. He had a boyish look with smooth skin and big blue eyes. He was wearing a navy-blue suit with a white shirt and red tie. He looked every inch the businessman.

"My name is Sebastian, and I'm the head of product management. I will actually be working with two of you directly, so I look forward to seeing who is part of my team. Do any of you have experience with product management or marketing?" He looked around the room, and a few of the girls raised their hands.

I wanted to put my hand up as well, but I was scared that he'd asked me a question I couldn't answer, that I'd look like a fool. However, he definitely looked like the sort of guy that I would want to work for.

"Okay, well, I'll be back a little bit later. I just wanted to come and say hi before the day started, and Gloria, be kind. We do need all of these employees."

"I'm just doing my job, sir."

"I know," he grinned, "but we are in need of personnel, so let's not get rid of too many people on the first day."

"Yes, sir," she said.

"You're welcome, ladies." He winked at us before he waved and left the room again.

I smiled as he walked out. I was really hoping that I could get a position with him. I had a feeling he'd be one of the nicer bosses to work for. Unlike the other girls, I had no interest in working for the CEO. By all accounts, he was old and grumpy and mean. Plus, if you were working for the CEO, you'd always have lots of work, and I liked my downtime. I liked to surf the internet and sometimes read books on my Kindle, and I knew that wouldn't fly if I was working for the big boss himself.

FIVE

"Hey, Susie. Are you there? I'm on my lunch break."

"How's it going?"

"Honestly?"

"Of course, girl, honestly."

"I don't know how long I'll be at this job."

"What? What do you mean? You barely started."

"Yeah, and now I know why they hire so many temps. It seems like they fire people for basically breathing."

"Is that why you're whispering on the phone?"

"Yes," I said, laughing slightly. "I'm outside a block away, and I'm on my lunch break, and I'm still nervous that Gloria's going to find me and tell me off."

"Who's Gloria?"

"She's in charge of HR, or she's in charge of the new hires for the HR department. I'm not exactly sure. All I know is that she reminds me of that mean old lady in *Matilda*, and she walks around with a clipboard like she thinks she's a sergeant in the Army or something."

"Oh, boy," Susie said. "So I'm guessing that I don't have a temp job there as well?"

"Yeah, sorry. You can still apply at ABC Temps, though—"

"I don't think so. If you're not liking it, then I don't think I'll like it either. Yeah, honestly, I would look for something else if I was you."

"But there is some good news."

"Ooh, what?"

"See if you can guess."

"They're paying you $50 an hour instead of $25?"

"I said good news. I didn't say that I won the lottery."

"Well, you won the lottery the other day."

"Girl, I won $20."

"I know, but it was better than nothing"

"Yeah, true. But no, I'm not getting paid more than I thought. I wish. If they do take me on full-time, though, I would get a raise."

"Okay, so maybe you'll get taken on full-time."

"We'll see. I'll be lucky to make it throughout the rest of the week, to be honest."

"Okay, so tell me your news."

"There's this gorgeous guy that works here."

"You work at Winchester enterprises. I'm sure there are many gorgeous men that work there."

"Yeah, but this one came into the room and he was really friendly, and he didn't seem like a stuck-up asshole."

"Was he *really* good-looking though?"

"Yeah, he was cute. Why?"

"Because we both know if he's really good-looking, you're not going to give him the time of day."

"He was good-looking, but he also seemed nice. I just don't like when they're good-looking and cocky because—"

"I know, I know," Susie cut me off. "So, you got a date with this guy or what?"

"No." I laughed. "I wish. He came in, told us his name was Sebastian, and that some of us would be working on his team."

"Ooh, so you technically might date your boss."

"Well, I don't know if he's going to be my boss because I don't know if I'll be on his team, but I guess I wouldn't mind going on a date with my boss."

"Girl, do not mix business with pleasure. Trust me."

"What? That was when you were in high school."

"Yeah, and we both know what happened. " She made a face.

"Who told you to make out with your manager during rush hour at Burger King?"

"What, how was I to know that the general manager was going to stop by and that we'd be caught in the back fridge and both be fired on the spot?"

"I mean, I guess you wouldn't know unless you were psychic, but—"

"Oh," Susie interrupted, "guess what?"

"What?"

"I actually think I might have a job."

"What? No way! That's amazing."

"Well, it's not that amazing because it's telemarketing, but it does seem to pay well, and we really need the money."

"Oh, what sort of telemarketing? I—" I looked at my watch. "Oh, girl, I've only got seven minutes left. I need to go. I'm so sorry. I want to hear all about your job, but I also don't want to lose my job on the first day. Can we chat later?"

"Sure," she said. "I can't wait till you get home to hear more about Sebastian."

"Well, hopefully, you'll hear that I'm working for him." I laughed. "Okay, got to go." I hung up quickly and turned around. As I turned around, I bumped into someone.

"Oh my gosh, I'm so—" I looked up, my eyes widening as I recognized the guy from the bar.

He smiled at me. "Why, hello there, Marcia."

"Oh, hi. And goodbye. Sorry."

"Where are you rushing off to?"

"I have to get back to work."

"Oh yeah, I forgot. You work at Winchester Enterprises, right?"

"Yes, I do."

"And you are the head of marketing?"

"Yes, I am." I chewed on my lower lip. *Please, God, don't let Gloria walk by right now.*

"So what's the rush? Don't you set your own time? Surely no one's going to get upset at the VP of marketing for being a minute late on her lunch hour."

"I have a meeting right now, a very important meeting, actually, with the vice president of..." I looked and saw a guy selling hot dogs and sodas.

"The vice president of what?"

"The vice president of soda," I said quickly. "Ha ha. Actually, I can't really tell you because it's a secret."

"Your meeting is a secret." He raised an eyebrow. "Do you work for Winchester Enterprises or the CIA?"

"Well, if I told you, I'd have to kill you." I forced a light laugh. "But anyway, it was nice seeing you. Not. I have to go."

"What's the rush?"

"I told you." I looked at my watch. I had four minutes left. "I'm really sorry to bump into you, but I have to go."

"It seems like you just took an instant dislike to me, huh?"

"What? I said, staring into his bright green, laughing eyes. "No, I wouldn't say that—"

"I think so. The first time at the bar, you didn't want to chat."

"I was with my friend."

"And then when I came to give you your credit card back—"

"I said thank you."

"Yeah, but you weren't interested in—"

"And I'm not interested now. Have a good day, sir.

"You too, Marcia. You too. Perhaps we'll see each other again," he said with a little wave.

"I don't think so." I started running towards the building. I didn't even care if he saw me. I was much more scared of Gloria than I was worried about him seeing me running away. He could think what he wanted.

I was surprised that I'd seen him, though. How often do you see the same person randomly in a mere couple of days in New York? But it didn't matter.

He'd looked really handsome, though, and if I hadn't sworn off really handsome, cocky guys, I might have given him a shot. But I wasn't going to give him a shot. I might give Sebastian a shot if I had the chance, but not him.

I sighed with relief as I walked through the doors of Winchester Enterprises and waved to Shantal.

"Hey, Marcia." She waved back. "Want to grab a drink after work?"

"Sure," I said, "but I've got to get back now so that Gloria doesn't fire me and I lose my job on the first day."

"No worries," she said. "She likes to scare people."

"So she doesn't fire people then?" I asked, hopeful.

"Oh, no. Trust me, she fires people." Shantal rolled her

eyes. "But when you're done, come and meet me. I'll be here."

"Sounds good," I said.

"And if you want to invite anyone else, let them know."

"Will do." I gave her a smile and then hurried back to the conference room. I was the last temp to get there, but fortunately, Gloria hadn't arrived yet.

Lilian smiled at me. "Hey," she said. "Where did you go for lunch?"

"I just actually took a walk and called my friend." I shrugged. "I don't really have lunch money. I'll probably have to bring a sandwich tomorrow if I still have my job."

"Ah, yeah. Sounds about right." She grinned. "I don't really have money to be eating out either. But you do know they have a cafeteria here where we get to eat for free."

"No way. We do?"

"You weren't listening to Gloria?" Lilian laughed.

"I must have slept through that part," I admitted, and we both laughed. "Hey, by the way, Shantal, the recep-tionist at the front, she said she's going to go for a drink after work if you want to come."

"I do." Lilian nodded. "But how can you afford to go for a drink if you can't afford lunch?"

"I can always find money for alcohol." I laughed, and then pressed my lips together quickly as Gloria walked in, a stern expression on her face.

She swept the room with a stern glance. "I'm glad to see that everyone is back from lunch on time. Now we're going to go through the handbook. This will take about two hours, so everyone, please make sure your phone is muted and put away."

I muted my phone quickly and placed it back into my

handbag, stifling a groan. How boring was it going to be to go through the handbook?

Gloria began to drone on about employee expectations, and my thoughts turned to the mysterious man I'd bumped into outside. I wondered if I would ever see him again. I didn't know why I cared or why he'd popped into my mind, but there was something about the way that his twinkling green eyes had looked at me that made me think that maybe I wouldn't be so upset if I were to see him just one more time.

Just so I could put him in his place, of course.

SIX

"Congratulations everyone." Gloria placed her clipboard on the table and clapped like she was at the opera. "You are officially a temporary employee of Winchester Enterprises. We will go to security to get your badges in a few minutes. First, I will let you know which departments you will be working in."

"Oh, awesome...I hope I'm with the hottie," Lilian said what we were all thinking.

"Sorry, what did you say?" Gloria frowned. "I didn't hear you properly."

"Nothing, Gloria." Lilian grinned wickedly and caught my eye. I smiled back at her but made sure not to get too excited. I didn't want Gloria changing her mind and getting rid of me. I hadn't scored very high on the Excel test, and I knew she'd been disappointed. My resume said I was a pro at Excel.

"So, Sarah and Maggie, you will be working in the accounting department, Lilian, you will be in product management, Wen and Maria, you will be in acquisitions, and Becky and Lawanda, you will be in social media."

"Uhm..." I cleared my throat, starting to feel nervous.

"Yes?" Gloria stared at me.

"I didn't hear my name."

"Oh, yes." Gloria looked pained. "You will be working in the executive office. So you will have another day of training."

"What?" I was shocked. "I thought you said the executive office doesn't take temps?"

"Normally, they don't." She sighed. "But it seems as if there is an urgent need for another assistant, and your skills fit."

"Oh?" What skills had the executive office seen on my resume that made them think I was a good fit? "Are they hoping to make a documentary of the company? Maybe a piece on the CEO?"

"I think not." She shook her head. "Mr. Winchester is very private, and you will likely have no contact with him. We will go over more information tomorrow." She picked up her clipboard. "Is everyone ready to go and get their photos?"

"Uhm, yes." I looked at Lilian, who was staring at me. "What?" I asked her.

"You lucky bitch," she mouthed.

"Huh?"

"Executive office? That's big money," she whispered as we stood up and headed towards the door.

"But I'm only a temp."

"But if you get through the first ninety days probation..." She rubbed her thumbs and fingers together. "Cha-ching!"

"Oh wow, but at least you got Sebastian." I sighed. "I wanted to be on his team."

"Yeah, he's a cutie." She nodded. "But I'd rather work for Finn Winchester." She licked her lips.

"Really? I saw his photo in the paper last year, and he looked like he was half bear, half Neanderthal."

"Oh really?" She giggled. "I guess he's into mountaineering, but girl, he's rich, really rich, I could do a mountain man, on the frigging mountain, for the sort of money he has."

I laughed. "I'm over the hotties anyway."

"Oh?" Lilian raised an eyebrow. "Sounds like there's a story there."

"Isn't there always?"

"Yup!" She nodded.

"Okay, everyone, fill out these papers." Gloria held up a stack of papers. "Leave them on the desk in the room. You can all leave after you get your badge from security. Arrive tomorrow at eight a.m., and I will escort everyone to their departments. Your department will then show you around the building."

"Yes, Gloria," I chorused with the other girls, excited that the day was nearly done. I grabbed my phone to text Susie.

Want to grab a drink with me and some of my new coworkers?

Sure? When?

I'm thinking in about an hour?

Sounds good.

:)

I put my phone back in my handbag quickly and waited in line to get my photo taken. I pulled out my pocket mirror and stared at my reflection before grabbing my lipstick and reapplying it. I then grabbed my powder and touched up my face. I didn't want my identity badge looking like crap.

"HEY, Shantal. Are we still on for a drink?" I asked my new friend as I approached her at the reception desk.

"Yeah." She smiled at me as she got up. "I am definitely in need of one. So how was your first day?"

"It went as well as could be expected," I giggled, "with Gloria on my ass."

"Tell me about it," Lilian said next to me.

"You're in the new training class as well, right?" Shantal asked.

"Yeah. Hi, I'm Lilian."

"Sorry, I completely forgot to introduce you guys," I said quickly.

"Oh, no worries. I'm going to join you guys for a drink if that's okay," Lilian said with a smile.

"The more the merrier," Shantal said. "I'm really glad that you guys are both down for it. So many people that work here just have a stick up their ass, you know?"

"Well, I sure don't," Lilian said. "I mean, I've had things up my ass before, but we're not going to talk about that until we have a couple of drinks." She grinned at both of us. "I hope that doesn't offend you."

"Doesn't offend me," Shantal said with a giggle.

"Not me either," I laughed. "Oh, and my roommate and best friend, Susie, is going to join us as well."

"Oh, of course," Lilian said. "Is she the one that you were hoping to get a job for?"

"Yeah. I had kind of said that maybe I'd have an in now that I was a temp, but obviously, that's not going to happen.

And after I told her about Gloria, she's not really interested in working at Winchester Enterprises anyway."

"Why not? It's such a great job," Shantal said. "I mean, don't get me wrong. It's not the job I was hoping to get, but it pays the bills."

"Yeah. That's what I need right now. I have not paid the bills in let's just say too long. And Susie has been going over our finances, and we're in really bad shape."

"Oh, no," Lilian said. "How have you guys paid rent? And how long have you guys been in the city?"

"We've been in the city for six months. And let's just say we no longer have any of our childhood savings left. Sorry, Grandma and Granddad!" I shrugged ruefully.

"Oh, I see how it is. So, you just moved from Florida?" Shantal said.

"Yep. I guess you could say I'm fresh off the boat. You know what I mean. Off the plane."

"Yeah, I get it," Lilian said. "I guess a lot of us come to New York City with dreams and hopes of making it, and we end up at a place like Winchester Enterprises. Oh, and by the way, Shantal?"

"Yeah?"

"You will have to give me all the tea on Sebastian."

"No, you're not on Sebastian's team, are you?"

"Yeah, yeah. Why?"

"He's gorge," Shantal said. "Everyone that gets on his team is super happy."

"And has he dated any of them?"

"No. He doesn't date anyone on his teams. He doesn't want to get in trouble. There's a no-fraternizing policy at Winchester. I'm surprised Gloria didn't fill you in on it." Shantal rolled her eyes. "She loves to go on about how you can't date anyone else that works at the office. As if. It's mostly women who work here."

"I was wondering about that," I said. "I mean, there were only women in our training class. And aside from Sebastian, I haven't seen many other men."

"Oh, there are men that work here," Shantal said, "but I think that men have egos and most men don't want to be assistants. I don't know."

"Yeah, men have egos all right," Lilian said. "You know, that's a huge problem if a man has a bigger ego than ..."

"Than what?" I interrupted her.

"I was going to say than I do. What were you thinking, dirty?"

"What?" I laughed and gave her my most innocent expression. "I was thinking exactly that."

"Uh-huh. You weren't thinking I was going to say a big—"

Shantal put her hand up. "I'd be happy to show you the offices tomorrow."

"Huh?" I tilted my head to the side. It was then that I saw Gloria walking past.

"Good evening, ladies," Gloria said, giving us a stern look. "I take it you will get a restful evening and not stay up too late watching TV seeing as you have to be at work tomorrow."

"Yes, ma'am," Lilian said.

"Yes, Miss Gloria," I said. She looked at me. "I mean, Gloria."

"Yeah, Gloria. See you tomorrow," Shantal said.

We waited until Gloria left the building and then we all burst into laughter.

"What do you think Gloria would've done if she'd heard me say big cock?" Lilian said with a giggle.

"She would've fired you," I said.

And Shantal nodded. "Yep, you definitely would've been fired."

"At least I would've been able to date Sebastian then," Lilian said with a smile. "So do you know where we're going to go, Shantal?

"Um, seeing as you guys are new, and we're all kind of broke, I was thinking we could go to Harpoon Hurricanes. It's this cool little bar about five minutes from here, and tonight they have $2 cocktails."

"Two-dollar cocktails. Really?" I stared at her in surprise. "I've never heard of a place that has $2 cocktails."

"Trust me, you'll like it," Shantal said. "I know all the good places with all the good deals."

"Okay. Well, let me text my friend, Susie, and tell her where to meet us."

"Sounds good," Shantal said. "And oh, yeah, of word of advice, you guys."

"I'm always open for advice," Lilian said.

"Yes, please," I added. "I need all the advice I can get."

"If you ever get asked to do any work for Mr. Winchester, try to get out of it. He's known for being a total slave driver." She shuddered. "I've never had to work for him, and no one I know has had to work for him. But everyone that has worked for him doesn't last at the company long. So if you need a paycheck ..." She made a face.

"Oh, no," I said.

"Uh-oh. What is it?"

"I got assigned to his executive team."

"You did?" Shantal's jaw dropped. "How is that even possible?"

"What do you mean?"

"No one gets assigned to the executive team unless they've been working here for at least a year. Especially not a temp. Wow, that's crazy." She looked at me. "Do you have connections or something?"

"No. I just got the job through ABC Temps," I shrugged. "I mean, this isn't even the job I was actually applying for."

"Oh. What job were you applying for?"

"You guys really don't want to know." I bit my lip as we walked down the street.

"Yeah, we do. Tell us."

"So I kind of was applying for the head of marketing position."

"Ouch!" Shantal made a face. "You applied for head of marketing and they made you a temp instead. Wow, you must have crazy degrees and experience, huh?"

"No." I shook my head. "Literally one bachelor's degree and not much experience. But I figured I know social media, right?"

"What?" Shantal's jaw dropped. "You're joking."

"No. What's that saying? You lose all the bets you don't make."

"Never heard of that one before," Lilian said cheerfully. "So, Shantal, she shouldn't take the job in the executive office?"

"I mean, it's unlikely that you're going to work directly for Mr. Winchester. He has an EA and his EA has an EA and his EA's EA has an EA. So you'll most probably be in a supporting role to one of them. But," she shrugged, "good luck."

"I know," I groaned. "I had a feeling it wasn't going to be great, especially because I have to go to another day of training tomorrow with Gloria. So I can't stay out long, and

I can't get drunk because I have to be here on time. I'm probably going to have to take copious notes and actually pay attention.

"You got this girl," Lilian said. "Trust me. If anyone's got this, you got it."

"Really?" I stared at her in surprise. "I thought I'd been one of the least attentive people in the day's training. Certainly not anyone that would make another new employee think that I was one of the best."

"I mean, I'm trying to be positive for you."

"Oh my gosh. I'm nervous. I can't afford to lose this job."

"Positive mental attitude, girl. You haven't lost anything," Shantal patted my arm. "And a word of advice."

"Yeah?"

"Don't let Gloria goad you into saying or doing anything that you can't back up."

"Huh? What do you mean?"

"You'll see," she said. "Trust me, you'll see."

SEVEN

"Don't look now," Susie said as she leaned forward.

"What?"

"But the guy that we saw the other day, he's at the bar."

"No way." This time, I knew better than to actually turn around and look. I definitely did not want to make eye contact with the green-eyed, cocky bastard I had now seen three times.

"What are you girls whispering about?" Shantal asked as Susie sat back.

"So," Susie grinned, "You want to tell them, or should I?"

"I'm not going to say anything. There's nothing to say." I looked around at my friends innocently.

"Okay, spill the tea," Lilian said. "I need some good information."

"There's nothing—"

"There's a guy that's got the hots for Marcia," Susie said, laughing.

"No, he doesn't!" I objected, but Lilian cut me off.

"Ooh, tell me more," she leaned in, looking eager. "You've been holding out on us."

"Trust me, I haven't. It's not anything. We went to have a drink a couple of nights ago, and there was this guy at the bar who was trying to interrupt our conversation, and I told him, 'Butt out, I'm not interested.' Then we were sitting at a table and he happened to come over because I left my credit card there. Once again, nothing happened. And then I was walking down the street yesterday and I bumped into him again."

"Wow, talk about serendipity," Shantal said. "So, did you guys exchange numbers? Did you—"

"No, we did nothing. He was really cocky, really full of himself—"

"Marcia, you don't even know him," Susie said. "She's not giving him a chance because her last boyfriend was really good-looking and a douche bag and a cheat, so now she's scared to date someone really good-looking."

"Ooh, so he's really good-looking, is he?" Lilian said.

"Yeah, he's really good looking and he's at the bar right now," Susie said.

"Ooh, where?" Both Shantal and Lilian looked towards the bar.

"Guys, you're making it so obvious."

"Um, sorry," Lilian said with a wicked grin. "Which one is he?"

Susie looked towards the bar and frowned. "Oh, well, I guess he's gone."

"Or maybe you didn't see him," I grumbled.

"Trust me, I saw him, and he definitely noticed you. I saw him looking over here."

"Oh, my gosh. I think this guy might be stalking me."

"Oh my gosh, I just had an awful thought." Susie's expression suddenly became serious.

"What is it?"

"So, what if he is a bill collector?"

"What?" I looked at her in confusion. "What are you talking about?"

"Girl, didn't you say that you haven't paid one of your credit card bills for a few months?"

"Yeah, but I called them and I told them I'm going to make a payment as soon as I get my first paycheck, and they said that's fine. They've got me on some plan. They said if I don't make the payment then they're going to send me to collections, which would suck, but I told them I should get my first paycheck in a couple of weeks, and they said as long as I pay by then it's going to be okay."

"Oh, okay," Susie said. "Well, I mean, you always hear about how sometimes these debt collection agencies send people."

"Oh, my God, that would just be my luck," I sighed. "Anyway, I'm going to go to the restroom. I'll see you guys in a second, okay?"

"Don't get lost," Lilian said.

"I'll try not to," I laughed and then looked at my watch. "And I should most probably get going right after that. I need to get my outfit ready for tomorrow and I really need to get a good night's sleep, because I cannot afford to be late."

"Aw, you don't want to stay for one more drink?" Lilian said.

"No. I'm going to go to the restroom, and then I'll come back and chat for a little bit, but then I'll leave."

"Okay."

I got up and made my way through the bar. It was absolutely packed. I assumed that was because they had a crazy special on their drinks for women, and the even crazier part was that they were using top-shelf liquor, as well. I had a feeling it was because they were attracting so many businessmen who were willing to pay crazy prices for the cocktails. I looked around for the restroom and I saw a line of women at the far back and I assumed that was where it was. I made my way to the back when I felt some fingers tapping on my arm. I looked up in surprise and that's then I saw him, Green Eyes himself.

"Are you following me?" I asked him before he could say anything.

"No. I was about to ask you the same thing."

"You were about to ask me if I was following you?"

"Yeah. You keep showing up everywhere I am."

"Uh-huh. Well, trust me, I'm not following you. In fact, I think it's kind of creepy that in a city this big, you seem to choose every bar that I go to and you just seem to be everywhere."

"Well, New York City isn't the largest city in the world. Perhaps we just like to frequent the same places."

"Perhaps." I folded my arms across my chest. "Anyway, can I help you?"

"Just wanted to see what a hotshot marketing guru was doing in a bar like this."

"I'm just having some drinks with my friends. You?"

"I just came to have a drink before I went back to the office to do some work, actually."

"You work in an office?" I looked him up and down. He was wearing a denim shirt with jeans. "Don't tell me you're on Wall Street?"

"No," he shook his head. "Not on Wall Street." There was a twinkle in his eyes that I found hard to resist. "So," he said, pausing slightly. "How long have you been a president at Winchester Enterprises?"

"Why are you so concerned about my job? I don't ask you about yours."

"I guess I've always been intrigued by women in powerful positions, and I'd love to know—"

"Dude, really? Is this your best pickup line?"

"My best pickup line?" He looked affronted. "Really? You think I'm trying to pick you up?"

"Let's be real here. You don't give a shit about what it's like for me to be in a position of power."

"I actually am very interested."

"Really? Or are you just trying to figure out my relationship with Finn Winchester?"

"Your relationship with Finn Winchester? I didn't know you had one."

"Well, obviously, he and I are very close, because I'm president of his company, and—"

"Oh, I guess that wasn't obvious to me, but please, do tell me more. What's he like?"

"What—what's he like?" I stammered. I wasn't sure why I had brought it up again. Maybe because I wanted him to feel intimidated. Maybe because I wanted him to feel like I knew men who were much more powerful than him, so he should back off.

"Yeah, I mean, if he's your boss and, from what I'm now gathering, your friend."

"He's really into mountaineering."

"He's really into mountaineering? Oh."

"Yeah. He loves to climb mountains. He was just at Everest and he was also at—" I paused, trying to think of another mountain.

"What mountain?"

"Mount Sinai."

"He was at Mount Sinai? Interesting. Where is that again?" He looked at me. I had a feeling he knew that I had absolutely no idea where Mount Sinai was, but maybe he didn't know, either. I was going to call his bluff.

"Mount Sinai is in Australia. Yeah, he loves Australia. He goes there quite frequently because his aunt actually lives in Australia now."

"Oh, really?" The man's lips were twitching. "His aunt lives in Australia, huh?"

"Yep, and he likes to visit her because he also likes kangaroos. That's actually his favorite animal. Please don't tell the press that, or he will know it came from me."

"Oh, so you're the only one that knows that Finn Winchester, CEO of the multi-billion-dollar Winchester Enterprises' favorite animal is a kangaroo?"

"Yes, because he told me one night late when we were working in the office on a very important project."

"Oh. Well, you see, this has been very insightful for me. So, he's climbed Mount Everest. He's climbed Mount Sinai. And he has an aunt in Australia that he likes to visit frequently because he loves kangaroos?"

"Well, I mean, it's not just because he loves kangaroos. I mean, he also loves other animals, and he's just really into Australia and, um, Tim Tams."

"Tim Tams?" He raised an eyebrow.

"Yeah. He's just really ... Anyway, I just don't have time to talk about this with you right now."

"Aw, too bad. So, what's your name?"

"You already know my name."

"I know, but I thought we could introduce ourselves as if we're meeting for the first time. I mean, maybe you could formally tell me your name, Marcia?"

"You literally just said my name."

"Okay, but ..." He shrugged. "I was just trying to be polite."

"Dude, I don't even know what your problem is."

"Marcia, I don't know what your problem is. You seem to have an attitude with me. Did your last boyfriend look just like me or something?"

"No. Why?"

"Because that's frankly the only reason why I could think that you're being like this with me."

"How am I being?"

"I mean you're being quite combative."

"How am I being combative? It's not like I hit you."

"True, you didn't. But I'm just trying to talk to you. We're both at a bar. We're both single."

"You don't know if I'm single or not, and I certainly don't know if you're single or not."

"And what's that supposed to mean?" He looked at my lips. "Do you think I'd be chatting you up if you weren't single or if I wasn't single?"

"Well, you don't know if I'm single, and you're a man, and lots of men chat up women whether they're single or not."

"So that's the issue, huh?"

"That's what issue?"

"Your last boyfriend cheated on you."

"I don't know where you're getting that from."

"I'm a very good reader of people, Marcia."

"Okay, well, good for you."

"There's something about you, you know?"

"Oh?"

"Yeah." He took my hand. "There's just something about you."

"Why are you holding my hand?"

"I don't know. Maybe I wanted to play mercy."

"Really? How old are you?"

"Are you asking because you want to know, or are you asking because you think I'm immature for suggesting we play mercy?"

"I don't know, maybe you'll ask me to play tic-tac-toe next."

"I actually find tic-tac-toe to be quite an enjoyable game, don't you?"

"This is absolutely ridiculous. I was going to the restroom, and then I need to go home, so as much as I've enjoyed this conversation—"

"Give me your number."

"Sorry, what?" I blinked.

"If you've really enjoyed this conversation, give me your number."

"I was just being polite. I didn't actually enjoy this conversation."

"Do you think I'm attractive?"

"No," I lied.

"Liar."

"Excuse me?"

"I think you're a liar, Marcia."

"Why, because I said I don't find you attractive?"

"Among other things," he grinned.

I didn't even bother to ask what he meant by that. He seemed the sort who liked to play games, and I was not interested in playing games, even though he was most probably one of the sexiest men I'd ever seen in my life and I'd have loved to kiss him.

Fine, I admitted to myself. I wanted to kiss him.

But I wouldn't sleep with him because I wasn't the sort

of person that could sleep with a man without catching feelings, and I definitely didn't want to catch feelings for Green Eyes. No thank you. Nope. I just needed to get out of the bar and pray that I never saw him again.

"So, Marcia?"

"Yes?"

"Do you want to know my name?"

I stared at him, considering the question. I did want to know his name, but knowing his name would make it too hard. Once I knew his name, I'd be able to Google him. I'd be able to find him on Facebook and everywhere else and figure out who he was and what he was doing with his life. And once I got in deep like that, then I would want to get to know him better, and he would be someone real to me instead of some stranger I just saw in the streets every now and again.

"No," I shook my head. "I don't."

"Okay, then. You're honest about one thing, at least."

"I'm a very honest person, thank you very much."

"I'm sure you are," he grinned. "I'm sure you are. Well, I guess I'll bid you adieu, Marcia Lucas."

"My whole name? You know my whole name?"

"You know that. I gave you back your credit card."

"You didn't have to read my credit card."

"For that, I'm sorry. But don't worry, I didn't memorize the credit card number. Don't worry, I won't be spending your sixty grand."

"My sixty grand? What are you—" And then I remembered the lie I told about my credit line. "Well, just so you know, if I see any charges on the credit card that I didn't make, I'm going to blame you."

"Okay, then," he nodded. "Well, have a good evening with your friends, Ms. Lucas. Until we meet again." He gave a little bow as if he were a butler in an old movie, and I couldn't help smiling. He was funny, I'd give him that.

"Well, you have a good evening, too." I turned around quickly and walked away. My heart was pounding but there was a smile on my face. He was handsome, and he was interesting, and he was funny. Part of me was tempted to walk back and ask for his name and number and tell him to give me a call sometime, but there was no point. I mean, where could we even go from here? I'd lied about my job, and I'd lied about my friendship with Finn Winchester. No, it was better for me to just keep things the way they were and move on with my life. I had other things to focus on and worry about. I didn't need to worry about some handsome green-eyed man who showed up in little dive bars in New York City. I'd have plenty of time in the future to worry about getting a boyfriend.

Now was not the time to complicate my life even further.

EIGHT

I lay in bed, staring at the ceiling. I should have been sleeping, but all I could think about was the green-eyed man from the bar. There was something unforgettable about his dazzling smile, and as I thought about his luscious pink lips, I wondered if I had made a mistake not asking for his name. I debated whether I'd acted like a scaredy-cat or whether I had been smart. Men like him could get any woman that they wanted. Men like him could break your heart in a million ways and walk away without looking back. But I knew I couldn't live my life being scared of dating and rejecting every attractive man I met.

I resolved that if I were to see him again I would ask him his name. I would go up to him and I would say, *Hey, this is Marcia. Remember me?* And he'd smile and say, *Of course,* because why would he say anything else? I smiled to myself at that thought. And then I'd ask him his name. And he'd say it was something exotic like Damian or Mario. And then he'd tell me he was a model or an actor or maybe he worked in a grocery store.

I laughed out loud at that thought. There was no way my green-eyed man worked at a grocery store.

I looked at my phone and groaned when I saw that it was two a.m. I had to get up in five hours. I definitely could not afford to be late. I wasn't sure how I felt about my job at Winchester Enterprises. I didn't want to tell Susie, but I wasn't sure I was going to be happy there. I mean, Lilian and Shantal were amazing, but if everyone else was like Gloria then it was going to be an awfully uncomfortable work environment.

I wanted to be out in the real world. I wanted to be with my camera I wanted to be shooting videos of people and asking questions and documenting lives. I wanted to be submitting my short films to film festivals. One day, I wanted to win an Oscar. I knew that was a long shot, of course.

I knew Susie wanted me to achieve my dreams as well, but I also knew she was worried about money—and she had every right to be. I was also worried. I didn't want to admit it to her, but I was nervous we would get evicted. I'd seen the landlord just a couple of days ago, and he'd told me that if we didn't get our rent in on time this month, he was going to give us thirty days to vacate. That was why I'd gone to the temp agency. That was why I'd sucked up my pride and accepted the first job I could find. I knew that I would much rather be a temp, hating my job, than to go back to Florida and live with my parents. I loved my parents, but I was an adult now. And I absolutely hated Florida. I wanted to be young, single, and living life in the big city with Susie.

So far, we hadn't really been able to do that, but we were on the right path. We already had two new friends. I knew that Shantal and Lilian were going to be longtime friends. The way that we bonded, the way that they made me laugh, the way that we all just seemed to gel. We were all new to the city, and we all had dreams and goals.

While I was nervous about the job and anxious about the rent, I was still optimistic. Things were starting to look up. Maybe everything was going to be okay. And maybe I'd be so excellent at the assistant position at the executive office that they'd offer me a permanent position even sooner than I thought.

I SHOULD HAVE KNOWN the training would be excruciatingly boring. Gloria had caught me yawning every ten minutes as she droned on about the hierarchy of all the different managers and different software programs that I'd never heard of before.

"What coding programs do you know?" Gloria appeared to be reading from a script. "Do you know C++ and Python?"

I had no clue what she was talking about. "Python like the snake?"

"The coding program." Gloria scribbled something on her pad. "Obviously that's a no."

"I mean, I can learn it if I need to." I had absolutely no interest in learning the program, but she didn't need to know that.

"So, Marcia, We're gonna have to have you take a vocabulary test today."

"Excuse me? Why do I have to take a vocabulary test?"

"Because that is one of the requirements of working for the CEO, Finn Winchester."

"I think it's derogatory and degrading that you're going to ask me to take a vocabulary test period. How come you didn't ask everyone else to take a vocabulary test?"

"Because no one else was working in the executive office."

"I didn't ask to work in the executive office, thank you very much. I would have much rather have worked with Sebastian and product management."

"Yes, I could see that, the way you were throwing yourself at him." Gloria gave me a disapproving look.

"This is absolutely ridiculous." I pressed my lips together before I said anything really regrettable.

"Oh and also..." She was silent for a few seconds.

I frowned, wondering why she looked so uncomfortable. Gloria didn't seem the sort of person who was uncomfortable saying or doing anything.

"Yes, what is it?"

"We're going to need you to sign a contract stating that you won't try and seduce Mr. Winchester."

"You *what?*" I stared at her. "You want me to sign a contract saying what?"

"I do believe that I spoke English, Miss Lucas."

"You want me to sign a contract saying I'm not going to *seduce Mr. Winchester?* Are you out of your mind? I have absolutely no interest in Mr. Winchester. I've never even met the man before in my life."

"Yes, well, Miss Lucas, Mr. Winchester is a very eligible bachelor, which I'm sure you know, and as such, we need to ensure that you will not try and get your hooks into him."

"I'm not interested in him. I saw him in the newspaper last year, and frankly, he looked like a beast. And I'm not one of those women that's interested in the Beast. I'd much rather have a handsome prince."

"I can assure you, Miss Lucas, that Mr. Winchester is no beast. He has dated the finest models from France and Milan—"

"Gloria, I couldn't care less who he's dated. Are you sure you're the one that's not trying to seduce him?"

"How dare you, Miss Lucas?" she gasped, looking deeply offended. "You will sign a contract stating that you will not seduce him. You will sign a contract stating that you will not fall for him. And you will sign a contract stating that you will not dress in inappropriate attire while you are at work in the offices of Winchester Enterprises. Do you understand?"

I stared at her in shock. I had never seen her so animated in the three days that I'd known her. Finally, I simply nodded. There was no point getting in an argument with her, and I didn't want to lose my job just because I didn't want to sign a contract about falling for a man I never even met before in my life.

"Miss Lucas, I need to hear an answer."

"That's fine, Gloria, if you want me to sign a contract saying that I don't want to bang Chewbacca then sure I will."

"Chewbacca?"

"You've never seen *Star Wars*?" I raised an eyebrow. To be honest, it didn't surprise me that she hadn't seen *Star Wars*. She seemed like the sort of person that only watched cooking and antique shows.

"Miss Lucas, I'm going to be quite frank with you. If it were up to me, you would not have even made it to the second day. However, your resume impressed someone in the executive office enough that I was ordered to ensure that you made it through the training process. But I'm going to tell you something. If you continue in the manner that you have begun, you will not last more than a month at this company."

I stared at her in shock. I wasn't shocked at what she'd said, because I believed her. I was actually surprised that I'd made it this far. What shocked me was the fact that someone in the executive office really wanted me to stay. What had I put in my resume that was so impressive?

I tried to remember what skills and qualifications I'd listed. I mean, there was nothing that special about me unless they really wanted someone with mediocre juggling skills, or the ability to balance ten books on my head without them falling off. I'd included those facts because I'd thought they'd make me stand out as someone with a good sense of humor, but I hadn't actually thought they'd be skills a corporation was looking for. But maybe they were. Maybe Winchester Enterprises was trying to get into the circus space. I mean, I didn't know why they would be, but it wasn't up to me what they decided to do with their money. Let them make shitty investments.

"When is this test?" I'd have to rush to the bookstore and get some SAT vocab books to brush up. And maybe a dictionary.

"In three days." Gloria smiled sweetly. "It will give you some time to prepare for the tests."

"Tests? As in multiple?"

"Oh, yes. We need to test the skills you list on your resume..." She gave me a pointed look. "We already know you exaggerated your Excel skills."

"I told you, I'm used to working on a Mac, not a PC. That's why I forgot some of the commands." I knew I was being insubordinate and was just waiting for the ax to fall.

"Certainly, Miss Lucas." Gloria headed for the door.

"You have a fifteen-minute break now." And with that she left the room, leaving me to wonder what I'd gotten myself into.

NINE

"Oh my gosh, Shantal. I am absolutely going to flip the script if Gloria does not get off my back." I walked up to my new friend as she sat behind the receptionist's desk chewing on a chocolate bar.

"Oh, no. What happened now?" She gave me a sympathetic look.

"Gloria just told me that I'm going to have to take a vocabulary test and that I have to sign a contract stating that I will not try and seduce Finn Winchester." I rolled my eyes. "I haven't even met the man, and she's worried I'm going to try and seduce him."

"No way!" Shantal's eyes went wide. "I've never heard of anything like that!"

"So ... this isn't normal, then?" I'd been offended, but I'd thought it was par for the course for people working in the executive office.

"Girl, I've never heard of anyone having to sign any sort of contract." She shook her head. "But then maybe you're going to have to sign an NDA as well," she shrugged. "And I guess if you sign an NDA, then technically you're not meant to be talking about it."

"Oh, boy. So does that mean I'm in trouble already?"

"Well, you haven't signed anything yet." She smiled. "Plus, you told me, and I'm not going to tell anyone. Well, no one that works here."

"Shantal, who are you going to tell?"

"I mean, I might tell my best friend, Benny."

"Your best friend, Benny?"

"Yeah, her real name's Bernadette. But she goes by Benny for obvious reasons."

"Obviously," I laughed. "Okay, and why would you tell her?"

"Because I tell her everything, and that's kind of funny."

"It's not funny. It's offensive! Like, who does Gloria think I am that I would try to fricking seduce Bigfoot?"

"Oh my gosh. He's not Bigfoot!" Shantal laughed. "You really haven't seen Finn Winchester?"

"Girl, I told you I saw him in the newspaper from when he was hiking."

"Yeah, but haven't you seen any other photos of him?"

I shook my head. "No, the only other photos I saw was when he was young with his family, and that doesn't really tell me much."

"Yeah, he is very private," she nodded. "Surprisingly, because he's always going out with—"

"Don't tell me. Models and actresses from Milan and Rome and London."

"Um, I was going to say he's always going out with famous women," she laughed. "What's up with the models and actresses from all those exotic destinations?"

"Oh, that's what Gloria said to me. I think she might be in love with him."

"That wouldn't surprise me," Shantal said. "Maybe that's why she's got such a stick up her ass."

"Tell me about it," I said. "So, you think he's cute?"

"I mean, he's not really my type." She shrugged. "But he's pretty fly for a white guy."

"Oh, Shantal. That's so funny."

"I mean, he's cute, I'm not going to lie, but it's not like we run in the same circles, right?" She shook her head. "I sit at the front of the office as the receptionist. He's upstairs in the executive suites with champagne and caviar in his fridge."

"He has champagne and caviar in his fridge?"

"I don't know," she shrugged. "I just mean it's two different worlds."

"I mean, I thought I knew people who had money when I was in Florida, but not like Winchester money. I guess he's, what? A millionaire?"

"Girl, I think he's a billionaire if the newspapers are right. And if the whisperings around the office are correct."

"Oh, what are the whisperings around the office?"

"Well, let's just say that one of the reasons why the executive office is looking for someone so badly is because..."

"Oh my gosh, he slept with his last assistant?" I rolled my eyes. "Well, there you have it."

"No, girl. He didn't sleep with her, but—"

"Oh my God, what? They had a one-night stand."

"Girl, a one-night stand would be sleeping with her."

"I know, but—"

"No, just listen. So, at the Christmas party, she left Mr. Winchester a note that said meet me in some office."

"Okay."

"Well, she had a plan to seduce him."

My eyes widened. "Okay, go on."

"So she's in there, waiting. The lights are out, and she hears the door open."

"Okay." I lean forward eagerly. "What happened next?"

"Well, she hears a cough, and it's male. So she grabs him. He tries to say something, but she puts her hand over his mouth and she starts kissing him."

"No way!"

"Yep." Shantal was grinning now. She leans forward and whispered, "And then..."

"What?"

She looks around. "I don't know if I should really say this."

"Oh my gosh, you cannot start a story like this and then stop!"

"Fine, but I'm not really meant to be engaging in office gossip sitting at the front of the building representing the company."

"Really, Shantal? You sit here gossiping all day long."

"I know," she grinned. "But trust me, when my bosses are around, I have to look professional."

"I know, but hurry. I've only got five minutes before I have to get back in the office."

"Well, let's just say Jane—"

"Who's Jane?"

"Jane's the assistant that left the note in the office."

"Okay, okay."

"Jane wasn't wearing any panties."

"Whoa. Okay."

"And let's just say she was wearing a dress, and she lifted the dress up and stuck his hand you know where."

My jaw dropped. "No, she didn't!"

"Yes," Shantal snickered. "Yes, she did."

"Oh, shit."

"And let's just say they had sex."

"She had sex with Finn Winchester in a dark office, and he didn't even know who she was?"

"Well, that's what the story would have you believe, right?"

"Um, yeah. That's the story you just told me, Shantal."

"Yeah well, get this. Jane ends up pregnant."

"No way," I said loudly and then clamped my hand over my mouth. "Oops, sorry. Oh my gosh, so then what happened?"

"So then she goes to Mr. Winchester's office."

"Okay."

"And she has a pregnancy test."

"Okay."

"And she tells him."

"Oh my gosh, what? What?"

"She tells him, 'Excuse me, Finn.'" Shantal puts on a snooty accent.

"Yes, and?"

Shantal started laughing.

"Oh my gosh. What? Tell me."

Shantal was laughing so hard now she could barely talk. "She says, 'Excuse me, Finn. You are the father.'"

"No way. So he had a baby with his assistant. Did he even realize it was her?"

"Girl, no. Get this. This is the best part of the story."

"Um, okay. What?"

"It wasn't Mr. Winchester that went into the office that day at the party."

"What?" This was like something on television. "No, please tell me you're joking."

"No, girl. It was the janitor!" Shantal started laughing hilariously.

My eyes felt like they were about to pop out of my head. "What? No."

"Yeah, girl. She slept with the sixty-five-year-old janitor. He nearly had a heart attack when he found out."

"What? Oh, my gosh. How did he find out?"

"So basically, when Jane went into the office with the pregnancy test, obviously Mr. Winchester had no idea what she was talking about. So she explained how she'd left the note for him and he'd come and met her after the Christmas party, and he told her that he'd never seen any note. So anyways, they finally figured out that the janitor had cleaned up the desk and the office and had seen the note. He went to go and talk to her because he thought that she was putting herself out there in a disrespectful way." Shantal grinned. "Well, I guess he felt like it was okay for her to be disrespectful with him."

"Wow. So then what happened?"

"Well, obviously Jane and the janitor both got fired. But get this."

"There's *more*?"

"Guess who the janitor was actually dating?"

"Um, I don't know. Finn's sister?"

"No."

"Mr. Winchester's mother?"

"No, girl. He was dating *Gloria*."

"Oh, no way." I couldn't believe it. I stared at her in shock. I didn't know what surprised me most, that Gloria was dating a janitor or that she dated at all.

"Girl, I don't know what happened. But yeah, it was absolutely crazy. Gloria was pissed, and I guess that's why she has an attitude now and is trying to make you sign a contract."

"This is absolutely ridiculous. So now she just hates anyone that works in the executive office."

"I guess so." Shantal shrugged. "But yeah, um, that's what you're dealing with."

"Girl, why didn't you tell me this before?"

"Well, I didn't think about it before."

"Girl. How did you not think about it before? That was juicy."

"Oh, trust me, Marcia. You ain't heard juicy yet." She grinned, and then she looked at her phone. "Girl, what time were you meant to be back in the office?"

"Um, at noon—Oh, shit," I interrupted myself. "I'm late. Okay, I got to go. I'll speak to you later. Bye, girl."

"Good luck," she called after me as I ran to the back room. I was breathing heavily when I reached it.

Gloria was standing at the desk frowning. "You're late. I told you you had fifteen minutes. You've been gone twenty minutes."

"I'm sorry. I—"

"You were up at the front gossiping again, weren't you?"

"No, I was—"

"I saw you, Miss Lucas."

"I'm sorry. And I'm sorry about everything else."

"Excuse me?" Her eyes narrowed as she stared at me.

"I understand now why you want me to sign the contract. I was a bit offended previously, but now I understand."

Gloria rubbed her forehead, took a couple of deep breaths, and then stepped towards me. "I don't think I know what you're talking about, Miss Lucas."

"I'm saying that I understand why you might think that I, as a young, somewhat attractive woman, might be a—"

"Miss Lucas," she interrupted me. "I don't care if you're young, or if you think you're attractive." She gave me a derisive once-over. I felt myself shivering slightly at her glance. She could have worked in a prison, she was that austere. "I'm going to make one thing very clear to you, Miss Lucas."

"Yes, Gloria."

"I did not come up with the idea for the contract." She stared right into my face. "I couldn't care less about you having a contract. In fact, as I've let you know previously, I don't even think you're right for this position—or any position—at Winchester Enterprises. However, this has come directly from the CEO."

"What?" My jaw dropped. "What do you mean it's come directly from the CEO?"

"That's all I can say. He wants to make sure that it's very clear that you're not to attempt to seduce or come onto him in any way whatsoever. Now, are you ready to get back to work?"

"Yes, ma'am." I went and sat down at the table, feeling angry and annoyed. What the hell? Why would Mr. Winchester think I'd have absolutely any interest in coming onto him? Was the man absolutely crazy? I knew one thing was for sure. When I finally got to meet him, I was definitely going to put him in his place.

TEN

"Susie, I am so pissed off right now. I don't even want to have to go back to the office tomorrow because Gloria sucks, and obviously, Mr. Winchester sucks. Like, who the hell does he think he is that he thinks I'm going to try and seduce him?"

"I do agree that he sounds very egotistical, but I guess he is a billionaire, and I guess someone did try and seduce him already."

"I mean, yeah, but that wasn't me. I'm not Jane. I never even met her. She sounds like an absolute desperado."

"You know what I want to know?" Susie asked.

"No. What?"

"I want to know if she couldn't tell that she was with a sixty-five-year-old man as opposed to a young, hot—How old is Mr. Winchester again?"

"I think he's thirty-five. Why?"

"Well, do you really think a sixty-five-year-old man has the same sort of cock as a thirty-five-year-old?"

"Girl, I don't know. I've never been with a sixty-five-year-old man, and hopefully never will."

"What about when you're sixty-five?"

"Well, I mean, when I'm sixty-five, sure. But maybe I'll trade in my husband for a boy toy." I laughed.

She giggled. "You're so silly."

"I have to be. I'm just so annoyed right now."

"Well, I have an idea," Susie said. "Something I was reading about in a psychology book."

"What psychology book?" I stared at her in surprise. "I don't know you to read psychology books."

"Well, it wasn't technically a psychology book," she giggled. "It was an article in a fashion magazine I was reading that was about psychological stuff."

"That's very different, Susie."

"I know, I know. But listen, it said when something's upsetting you or you're feeling pissed off, instead of reacting, just write it down."

"What do you mean, write it down? Like in a journal?"

"Yeah. You can write it in a journal or on a piece of paper. You can write it as an email. In fact, they say that one of the best ways to let go of anger and hurt is actually to write a letter to the person."

"I'm not writing that guy a letter."

"You don't actually *send* the letter. You can even just draft an email and then delete it when you're done, or leave it in your drafts and just reread it."

"Um, I guess. That doesn't really sound like a great idea."

"Trust me. Supposedly, what it does is allow you to process your anger without actually saying something directly. After you write it down, you can see if you still want to proceed."

"I guess."

"So maybe, right, if you get angry or upset again, you can just do that."

"Okay, I'll be like, 'Gloria. You're a bitch.'"

"Well, is it really Gloria you have the issue with, or is it Mr. Winchester?"

"Well, I've never met Mr. Winchester, so it's Gloria."

"Yeah, but didn't Gloria say that it was Mr. Winchester that said you have to sign this contract?"

"Yeah, she did. But who knows? Maybe she was lying."

"Why would she lie? She doesn't seem like the type to mince her words."

"That is true," I agreed. "She has been quite clear about the fact that she didn't really want me to get the position, so I guess she probably would have told me if it was her that wanted me to sign the contract. I just think it's so rude. Like, what are they trying to say? That I'm a gold-digger just because I have no money?"

"Girl, don't take it on. Let's be real, right? There are gold-diggers all over the place."

"Yeah, but I'm not one of them.

"Yeah, but they don't know you, Marcia."

"I know. I guess that's upset me. And then having to take this vocabulary test and all these other tests."

"All what other tests?"

"I'm not sure exactly. I just figured I would focus on the vocab." I picked up the three books I'd gotten at Barnes & Noble.

Susie picked up one of the books and flipped through it. "Girl, I don't know what half these words mean, and I sure can't spell them. We can do flashcards if you want."

"How are we going to do flashcards for 5,000 words?"

"Well, I guess not," she laughed. "When's the test?"

"It's in two days. I've got time to prepare. Yay, me."

"Girl, you were always a good last-minute crammer. You can do this."

"Yeah, but you know I suck at vocabulary. Like, am I applying to be an English teacher here? What the frig?"

"I guess if you're going to be mailing letters and sending out emails?"

"There's spell check for that shit, and dictionaries, and thesauruses. I don't need to have to know to spell everything myself."

"I know. That's really quite annoying, and it seems so archaic." She shook her head. "But everything about Winchester Enterprises seems pretty archaic to me."

"Oh? Why'd you say that?"

"I don't know. Just a feeling I get. But who knows? Maybe you'll really love the other people you work with."

"I wish I was working with Shantal and Lilian."

"You are."

"Not in the same office. Like, I might be lucky to see them at lunch and after work."

"True. But maybe the people in your office are going to be amazing, and maybe Mr. Winchester's also going to be amazing."

"From what I hear, I'm not even going to have any direct contact with him. Literally, I'm going to be the assistant to one of his assistants," I sighed.

"Girl, I mean, let's be real. He had a Maury situation at his office, right down to the pregnancy test. I understand why he would go to such lengths."

"I guess so, but it just seems ridiculous. The whole thing seems ridiculous."

"I know. I wonder if the janitor and Jane are still together?"

"You asked me that before, and I have no clue. I'll ask Shantal when I see her."

"You could always ask Gloria," Susie giggled.

"Oh, hell no. Now you're just being mean."

"I know." She stood up. "Okay, I need to go and do the dishes."

"Hey, Susie?" I followed her to the kitchen.

"Yeah?" She looked back at me.

"The other day, you said you were going to tell me something about a job you were offered, but we forgot to talk about it."

"Oh, yeah." She made a face. "I don't really know if I'm going to accept it."

"Why wouldn't you accept it when we need the money?"

"I know, but this job just really doesn't seem like me."

"Being a temp doesn't seem like me."

"Yeah, but..." she sighed, "I don't know if I can do this."

"Oh, shit. What's the job?" I stared at her. "You didn't apply to be a stripper, did you?"

"Of course not.

"An exotic dancer?"

"Girl, stripping and exotic dancing are the same things."

"I mean, I know that, but I didn't know if you were going to say that they were two different things now that—"

"Now that nothing, Marcia. No, I'm not going to be a stripper."

"Are you going to work at, like, Hooters or something in some skimpy outfit?"

"No." Susie rolled her eyes. "I'm not."

"So then what is it?"

"I told you, it's like a telemarketing job."

"So? What's wrong with telemarketing?" I pause. "Oh shit, it's not it's not phone sex, is it? Are you going to have to be one of those phone sex operators?" I lowered my voice. "Hi, thank you for calling 1-800-IM-HORNY. How can I help you today?"

"Oh, Marcia, stop it." She hit me on the shoulder. "You're awful."

"So, are you going to be Dr. Susie Love, or is it Dr. Susie Sexy?" I teased.

"You're stupid, Marcia."

"I know. So tell me, what's the job that you got that you can't take?"

"Fine. It's to be a psychic, okay?"

"To be a what?"

"To be a psychic. You know, predict the future?"

"How are you going to get a job up as a psychic if you're not a psychic?"

"Exactly."

"Oh, so it's like a con."

"It feels like a con, yeah."

"Does it pay well?" I asked her.

"Does it matter if it pays well?"

"I mean, you could do the job for, like, a couple of weeks 'till you find something new."

"Girl," she sighed, "I just feel like it would be wrong to pretend that I'm psychic when I'm not."

"I mean, if people believe you're psychic, then that's on them."

"I guess. So you think I should take it?"

"I mean, if your heart is really telling you no, then don't, but if you think you could suck it up for a little bit, then take it, just until you can find something else. I, um, didn't want to tell you this, but I saw the landlord the other day, and he told me that he's going to give us notice to vacate within thirty days if we're late on our rent."

"What? But we're not going to have enough by ..." She paused. "Oh, gosh. I have to take it, don't I?"

"I mean, will that really make a difference?"

"Yes. We get paid weekly." She ran a hand through her hair. "Okay. I'll take it. But..."

"Yeah?"

"You'd better not mess up at Winchester Enterprises. You'd better pass that vocabulary test, and you'd better sign that contract."

"I will."

"And if Gloria or anyone else gets on your nerves, just write an email, get it out of your system, and continue on with your day."

"Fine. I will."

"Good," she said. "Now help me with the dishes."

"What? It's your night."

"Please, Marcia?"

"Fine," I said. "Want to play some music while we listen?"

"Sounds good to me."

ELEVEN

"Oh my gosh, how am I going to remember all these words?" I moaned as I walked towards Winchester Enterprises.

Today was the day of my vocabulary test. I thought the whole thing was demeaning, but seeing as I needed the money, I had to take it, and seeing as I'd made Susie take the job as a psychic, I couldn't really turn away from this opportunity. It was a paycheck, and I needed a paycheck.

"Okay, okay," I said to myself, "Excruciating. E-X-C..." I chewed on my lower lip. "Fuck it, fuck it, fuck it. Okay, okay. New word. Don't panic, Marcia. Don't panic. Here's an easy one: panic. P-A-N-I-C. Panic." I grinned to myself. "Okay, at least I've got that one."

I stopped outside of a coffee shop and decided to get myself a coffee and a donut. If I was going to have a test, I might as well be sugared up. I was going to need all of the energy I could get.

I walked into the coffee shop and looked up at the menu for a few seconds. I was debating between getting a mocha, a cappuccino, or a matcha latte. I didn't really like matcha, but it seemed like it was healthier for you.

"Cat got your tongue?" a deep, familiar voice said.

I looked up, surprised, into a pair of green eyes. "It's you."

"Yes, it's me. Are you following me, Marcia?"

"I was about to say the same thing." There were butter-flies in my stomach.

"Oh really? So, are you going to say it...?"

"Actually, no." I looked up at his handsome face. It was like fate. It was like a window of opportunity on a horrible day.

"... What's your name?" I asked.

"Um, what?" He blinked at me twice.

"What's your name?"

"You want to know my name now?"

"Yeah, I want to know your name. You offered to give me your name, and now I'm asking."

"What made you change your mind?"

"I guess I was just thinking that..." I paused.

"You were just thinking that I'm so adorably handsome that you couldn't resist, right?"

"... No, I was just thinking that if I ever bumped into you again, it would be nice to know your name so I could say, 'Hey, it's you again, X,' as opposed to, 'Hey, it's you again, Mr. Green Eyes.'"

"Oh, so is that what you call me in your head when you're in bed?"

"I don't call you anything in my head when I'm in bed."

"Oh, really? So where did Green Eyes come from?"

"It's just a way of describing you because you have green eyes."

"Uh-huh. I don't think of you as Brown Eyes."

"That's because you know my name's Marcia."

"I don't think of Marcia either."

"Then what do you think of me as?"

"I think of you as Miss Prim and Proper Lucas."

I snorted. "Why?"

"I don't know. So can I buy you a coffee?" he asked.

I looked at my watch. "Um, I would say yes, but I'm actually in a hurry. So I'm going to say no, but thank you for the offer."

"Why do you have to hurry?"

"Because I have to be at work, and it's a very important day for me."

"Oh, a lot going on in marketing?"

"Huh?" I remembered my lie. "Oh, yeah, yeah, yeah. We all have a meeting with, um, Mr. Winchester today, all the presidents of the company, and it's very, very important because, you know, we're going onto the stock market soon and—"

"What do you mean you're going onto the stock market soon?"

"Well, you know, he is doing an IPO or XPO... you know."

"No." His lips twitched like he might be on the verge of laughing. "I thought Winchester Enterprises was a private corporation. I thought Finn Winchester said he would always keep it private."

"Oh?" I stared at him, nonplussed, "I guess I must have missed that part." I shrugged, "You know I'm president of marketing, not president of accounting."

"Uh-huh," he nodded. "So, how is Finn, by the way?"

"Oh, he's great. I was just talking to him last night, and he was saying he's so happy that I stayed at the company that he's thinking about giving me a bonus, and would I rather have a paid trip around the world or a Tiffany's bracelet for $50,000."

"Wow," Green Eyes' eyes widened. "I didn't realize he was quite so generous."

"Yeah, I guess he's generous, you know, because he recently thought he was having a baby and—"

"He recently thought he was having a baby?" His brow furrowed. "You don't say."

"Well, please keep it hush-hush. It's actually not meant to be well known because it turned out that it was his ex-girlfriend pretending..."

"It turned out his ex-girlfriend was pretending to have his baby. But I'm taking it she wasn't?"

"Well, yeah. You know," I licked my lips nervously and looked around. I would have definitely gotten fired if anyone at Winchester Enterprises knew what I was saying. "But you know, that's his personal business. I really shouldn't be talking about it. What do you do for a living, anyway?"

"Uh, maybe we can discuss over dinner one night?"

"Um, I don't know..."

"What, you don't want to have dinner with me now?"

"I don't know. You still haven't told me your name."

"Come to dinner with me, and I will."

"How am I meant to come to dinner with you if I don't know your name?"

"Well, I have an idea. How's about you give me your phone number, and I'll text you?"

"You'll text me?"

"Yeah, or you could give me your email address."

"Um, I don't know." I knew this was a bad idea, but the guy did have gorgeous eyes, and he did have kissable lips, and what could it really hurt to go to one dinner with him? "Fine, here's my number." I grabbed a napkin, pulled a pen out of my purse, and scribbled down my number. "But you probably shouldn't contact me today or tomorrow because I have some tests and—"

"You have some tests?" He raised an eyebrow. "What sort of tests?"

"Oh … I mean I have some tests to give to some of my lower employees, and I really need to focus on that."

"I see," he said. "It really does sound like a busy week for you as president of marketing at Winchester Enterprises."

The way he said it made me believe that he didn't actually believe what I was saying. I mean, who could blame him? I sounded like an imbecile. But maybe on the first date, at the end of it, if it went well, I'd tell him the truth.

"So, I actually don't think I have time for this coffee now. It's been great talking to you—"

"But why can't you get your coffee?"

"I don't have time, and I really can't be late today. I'll see you later."

"Bye, Marcia," he said. "Can't wait for that dinner."

"Me too," I called over my shoulder as I ran out the door.

It seemed like every time I saw the guy, I was late for work. There was no way Gloria would understand if I was late today. I don't even think Finn Winchester himself could save my job if I was late today. I had to get there on time, and I had to ace these tests. Otherwise, I was history.

History, I thought to myself. H-I-S-T-O-R-Y.

TWELVE

I waved at Shantal as I walked into the office building, but she didn't even look at me. There was an odd vibe in the air but I couldn't put my finger on exactly what was different. I flashed my badge to the security guard and plastered a smile on my face as I entered the training room. I was surprised to see that Gloria wasn't there. In fact, the room was empty. I looked at my watch and saw that I was one minute late. I was flustered. Was this it, then? Was I done?

I made my way to the table and pulled out a chair but just stood there, not knowing what to do.

The door opened and I looked up as a young-ish man hurried into the room with two coffees.

"Hi, Ms. Lucas?" He flashed me a nice smile.

"Yes?"

"Hi, I'm Jasper. I'll be proctoring the exams today and going over the contracts." He had a slight accent, and I wondered where he was from.

"Oh, okay. So Gloria won't be here?"

"No, all contact with her is done." He handed me one of the coffees. "This is for you."

"For me?" I looked at him in surprise.

"Yes, a hot mocha." He nodded and then reached into his messenger bag. "And a bagel with butter and cream cheese."

"Oh, you didn't have to bring me anything...I was going..."

"No, it's okay." He smiled. "I've been notified that Gloria forgot to show you to the cafeteria and breakrooms. We have free coffee and snacks all day."

"Oh, wow, that's awesome."

"And if you stay after five, you can order in dinner, on the company."

"Wow, that's a perk." I grinned at him, studying his dark eyes and short haircut. "Are you in HR as well then?"

"No." He shook his head. "I'm with the executive office. I'm one of the executive assistants."

"Oh, wow. Cool."

"I'm also an attorney, so I'll be going over everything with you."

"Okay ..." I was shocked that an attorney would be an assistant.

"Yes," He laughed. "My parents weren't pleased when they heard I was going to be an EA." He smiled ruefully. "They hoped I'd be a partner by now in a top law firm. I went to Princeton for undergrad and then to Harvard for law school."

"Impressive." My eyes widened. I'd gone to a no-name state school and partied more than I'd studied.

"You're from Florida?" He took a seat at the table and placed his briefcase in front of him.

"Yes." I nodded. "Central Florida. My mom is Puerto Rican and my dad is Irish American. They actually both grew up in New York; that's where they met, but they moved to Florida before I was born."

"Interesting." He nodded. "My parents are Nigerian. They immigrated to the States when I was four. They actually moved back a few years ago, but my sister Kemi and I still live here."

"Oh is that your accent, then?"

"It's a mix of Nigerian, English, and American." He laughed. "I went to boarding school in England from ages thirteen to seventeen."

I studied him, trying to figure out why such an accomplished and successful man worked here as an assistant. And how in hell had I gotten a position in the same office as him? My book-balancing skills were certainly not that impressive. "When I was in college, I took an African history class, and we learned about there being two tribes in Nigeria," I put in, wanting to say something.

"Yes, the Yoruba and the Igbo." He looked faintly impressed. "My parents are Yoruba. In fact, my grandfather was a chief in our tribe."

"Wow." I smiled, feeling sheepish. "Sorry, I keep saying wow. My vocabulary probably doesn't seem very impressive right now, does it?"

"Don't worry, Ms. Lucas." He smiled at me

"You can call me Marcia."

"Thank you." He took a sip of his coffee. "Please eat your bagel and relax. I will get all the paperwork ready."

"All the paperwork?" I took a sip of the most delicious coffee I'd ever had in my life. "Oh my, this is amazing."

"Kenyan beans." He grinned. "My country is superior, but the Kenyans, they grow some good coffee."

"This is to die for." I took another sip and closed my

eyes, relishing the rich coffee. I had no idea what was going on, but I wasn't going to complain.

"So would you like to do the vocabulary or the algebra test first?"

"Sorry, what?" I sputtered and coffee dribbled down my chin. I wiped it away quickly and stared at Jasper. "Did you just say algebra?"

"Yes." He nodded seriously. "Mr. Winchester wants you to take a vocab test and an algebra test. He also wants me to go over a list of to-do's for that position." He cleared his throat and looked down. "And a list of not-to-do's."

"Not-to-do's?" I raised an eyebrow.

"Yes, Mr. Winchester is concerned that you may try and make a pass at him or fall for him, and he just wants to ensure you know that this job is not an invitation to anything inappropriate."

I took another sip of coffee while I collected my thoughts. "I'm sorry, but is that really necessary? Don't I have to sign a contract saying I won't seduce him as well?" I rolled my eyes.

"Technically the list of to-do's is contained in the contract. We just need to ensure you understand." He cleared his throat. "If there is anything that is unclear, you may retain your own attorney."

"With what money?" I grimaced.

"Of course, we would pay." He smiled apologetically. "Sorry, I know this is highly unusual, but Mr. Winchester is very particular."

"He sounds like a paranoid ass—" I pressed my lips together and tried again. "I've never even met the man, and frankly, I don't know why he thinks I would want him. I can get a man much better looking than him. He can only wish I'd be interested."

"Well, Ms. Lucas, I certainly understand your sentiments, but if you wish to continue with your employment, you will be required to take the tests and sign the forms."

"Continue my employment?" I raised an eyebrow. "Technically, I haven't even started yet. I'm sorry, but this is ridiculous."

"I understand." He sighed. "Marcia, would you like to continue...?"

I bit my lower lip. I needed this job. "Yes. Do you have a computer I can use? I'd like to send an email real quick."

"Sure, in fact, I will take you to your office." He stood up. "You can take the tests there as well, and we'll go over the paperwork later this afternoon."

"Okay, sure. Let's see this office." I offered him a weak smile.

"It'll be okay, Marcia. I'm sure you will love it here."

"I sure hope so."

"Also, hablas español?"

"No." I shook my head. "I never learned Spanish. I wish I did though. I blame my mom for that. Do you speak Spanish?"

"Si," he grinned. "Bienvenido a Winchester Enterprises, señorita Marcia Lucas. Puede que no conozcas a mi jefe, pero parece conocerte. No tengo ni idea de por qué te va a hacer estas ridículas pruebas, pero no lo cuestiono. Eres una dama muy hermosa y si yo fuera tú huiría muy rápido. Tengo la sensación de que el Sr. Winchester va a ser una mala noticia para ti. Sin embargo, estoy seguro de que no entiendes nada de esto."

"Sorry, what?" I blinked at him.

"Oh, nothing." He shook his head and smiled. "Just an old Spanish poem I know."

I stared at him for a few seconds. I knew he was lying,

and he knew I knew, but there was nothing else I could say. He'd said something about Winchester Enterprises and possibly Mr. Winchester, but I had no idea what.

"Let me take you to your desk. I'll let you settle in, and then I'll be back to administer the tests."

"Thank you." I stood up, grabbing my coffee and bagel. I really wanted to call Susie, but I'd have to wait until I left the office. For all I knew, the rooms were bugged, and I still had bills to pay.

MY OFFICE WAS BEAUTIFUL. I had a view of the Manhattan skyline, and I could see the Chrysler Building in the distance. I hadn't expected to get my own office. It was small, but I loved it. A pinewood desk stood in front of the window. On the table sat a new Mac desktop computer and some files. There were some prints of Edward Hopper paintings on the walls, and I immediately felt a kinship with the room. Edward Hopper was one of my favorite painters, right after Picasso.

I sat in the large black ergonomic chair and spun around. I felt like an executive, and I loved it. I couldn't imagine what it would feel like to be someone with real power. It would definitely go to my head. I turned the computer on and spun around in the chair, then I jumped up and looked out the door to see if I could see anyone. There was a buzz of chatter in the air, but everyone was in their own offices. I pinched myself to make sure that everything was real. This was absolutely insane. I walked back to my desk and grabbed my phone so that I could text Susie.

I have an office.
No way!

Yes! And it's gorgeous.

Send pics!

Okay. Hold on. I took a photo behind the desk, showing the windows and New York skyline, and sent it to her.

WOWOW!!

Right? I grinned at her message. I was about to take a selfie in front of the window when someone knocked on the door. I placed my phone back on the table and turned around.

"Hi, Marcia right?" Sebastian stood there smiling at me. "I wanted to welcome you to Winchester Enterprises."

"Thank you!"

"Shantal mentioned you'd hoped to have been placed on my team."

I groaned inwardly—what else had she told him?—but forced a bright smile. "Oh, she did?"

"She said you were really interested in product management and sales?" His gaze was inquisitive, and I stared at him blankly. "We have some new products coming on the market in our pet retail space in the next quarter, so we will be looking for more team members then if you think you'd be interested?"

"Oh, yes. Sounds great." I beamed even though I had no idea what he was talking about. He really was quite handsome, though. I wondered if I could go on dates with Green Eyes and Sebastian? That would be naughty, but fun, and it wasn't like they would ever know. "There's so much for me to learn. Like, does anyone ever get together for drinks after work?" *Like, will we ever go for drinks after work?*

"Yes, there's a Happy Hour every Friday." He grinned. "You should definitely come sometime."

"Sounds good to me."

"Well, I should get going and let you get back to your work."

"Bye, Sebastian." I gave him a little wave and headed back to my seat. This day was really starting to go perfectly. And then I remembered the tests, and all happiness left my body. There was a very real possibility that I would fail these tests, and then I would be out of a job and out of a Happy Hour flirt with Sebastian. I idly played with the mouse and the screen in front of me came to life. An icon popped up that told me an email account had been set up for me. I clicked in and was taken to my Winchester mail account. I stared at the screen for a few seconds, feeling sorry for myself, and then remembered why I'd come here in the first place. Susie had said I should write out my feelings in an email to get it out of my system. I knew if I went into the tests with this level of anxiety, I wouldn't be able to focus.

I took a deep breath and typed out an email to the CEO of Winchester Enterprises, Finn Winchester.

TO MY NEW BOSS,

YOU ARE AN ASSHOLE. Maybe I will even call you a boss hole. We've never even officially met because you're worried all of your lower assistants will "fall for you and make a pass." You sent your executive assistant to give me a list of "to-do's" that were so basic I thought I was in preschool. And let's not talk about your "never-do's." You could only wish I would make a pass. You would be so lucky as to even catch a glimpse of my fine ass. In fact, why don't you kiss it, instead? Jerk.

Also, no, I'm not taking a vocabulary or algebra test. Just because you're the CEO doesn't give you the right to be pompous and arrogant. And frankly, I saw that photo of you in the newspaper last year; are you cousins with the yeti? Not a good look.

You can keep your $25 an hour. My self-respect is worth more than that. And no, I'm not interested in any of your other offers.

Marcia "I have self-respect" Lucas

P.S. Never in a million years would I ever try and seduce you, asshole.

I SAT BACK, chuckling as I reread the email. It felt good to get it all out. He was an asshole and obviously a cocky jerk if he had new assistants sign a contract saying they wouldn't seduce him. Just because one assistant had tried to trap him didn't mean everyone was interested in him. I hadn't even met the man—and frankly, had no interest in meeting him, either. I was just about to delete the email when Jasper walked back into the office.

"Hey, Marcia," he walked up behind me, "ready for those tests?"

"Uhm, yup." I clicked blindly to minimize the screen so that he wouldn't see the email I'd typed up. I turned to look at him, my face feeling hot. That had been too close for comfort. I couldn't imagine what he would have said if he'd seen my email to the big boss. I would have died. It wasn't like it was for anyone else's eyes, but he wouldn't have known that.

"So I thought we could discuss the setup and then..." He frowned. "Is something wrong?"

"No, why do you ask?" I was trying to control my breathing, and I might have been sweating a little. I felt like my entire body was betraying my guilt to Jasper.

"You keep blinking like you have a twitch or something." He paused. "Oh no, it's not medical, is it? I'm so sorry for commenting. I should have known better—"

"No, no." I cut him off quickly. Could this situation get any more embarrassing?

"Oh, good." He smiled. "Shall we sit?"

"We're taking the tests here?" I looked back at the computer screen.

"Uhm, yeah, that's why I showed you to your office. Are you sure everything is okay, Marcia?"

"Yes, I just got a little nervous. That's all."

"Don't be nervous." He smiled. "I promise you will pass."

"I sure hope so." I took a couple of deep breaths and then sat down. "Sorry, about my nerves. I've always tested poorly, and I really want this job, so I didn't want to fail."

"You got this, Marcia."

THIRTEEN

"Drinks are on me tonight." I was positively gleeful as I entered the bar with Susie, Shantal, and Lilian. "I passed the test with flying colors!"

"Congratulations!" Shantal grabbed my hand and spun me around. "Party time!"

"Well, I don't know about that. I still have to work tomorrow." I laughed. "You guys go and grab a table, and I'll order a pitcher of sangria."

"Sounds good," Susie answered.

The girls went to find seats, and I made my way to order the drinks. I half expected to see Green Eyes there and was slightly disappointed when I didn't. I pulled my phone out of my handbag and checked it yet again to see if he had sent me a text yet. My heart thudded as I noticed I had a new message from an unknown number. My fingers quickly tried to unlock my screen and I cursed under my breath as I got the code wrong three times in a row. Why did they make the numbers so small? Did they think everyone had children's hands? Finally, I unlocked the phone and read the message.

Hey big shot, executive. How was your day? I laughed at his message, even as my stomach sank. Where could this relationship even go if it was already starting with a huge lie?

Pretty good, thanks! I'm guessing this is Green Eyes?

Bingo! So you closed any multi-million deals today?

Just seven. No biggie.

No wonder Finn Winchester is so rich. It's all because of you.

I like to say a good 10% of his fortune is due to me. :)

You're too modest.

I know.

So what are you up to?

Drinks with the girls.

Ditch them and come and join me for dinner.

I can't do that.

You're a hot-shot executive. You can do anything you want.

Well, that's true. What do you do by the way?

Come and meet me, and I'll tell you.

Oh, like your name?

Yeah!

Well, I can't come.

:(Please?

Maybe in an hour.

I got the pitcher and carried it to the table where my

friends were sitting. "Would you guys kill me if I ditched early?"

"Why are you ditching?" Susie raised her eyebrows suspiciously at me. "You're not going shopping for new shoes, are you?"

"No, but I might have a date."

"A date?" Shantal sounded even more excited than I felt. "Who with? I didn't know you had anyone!"

"I don't have anyone. I just met this guy the other day. Well, several times..." My voice trailed off as I noticed that Susie was beaming. "Why are you grinning like a fool?"

"I'm just happy you're following your heart."

"My heart?" I raised an eyebrow at her and shook her head. "I don't even know the guy. I'm just following my way to a free drink and possibly a good makeout sesh."

"Just a makeout?" Lilian sipped her martini. "I'd at least want the guy to go down on me."

"On the first date?" Susie and I said in unison, and we both laughed.

"I see why you two are best friends." Shantal tapped her fingers against the table, in time to the beat of the song playing in the background. "Frankly, I would love to go on a date. I haven't met a good guy in years."

"I didn't even think they existed anymore," Lilian added.

"Guys, I don't even know if Green Eyes is a good guy." I stared at my phone to see if he'd sent another message. "I don't even know his name."

"How mysterious and sexy." Shantal sighed dreamily. "It's like the beginning to a movie..."

"On Hallmark?" Susie offered.

"No." Shantal grinned. "I don't watch those saccharine

movies. Like, have you noticed that the same ten actors and actresses are in every movie?"

"Yes." Susie laughed. "It's like they were all dropped off on an island."

"Not an island. A small quaint town somewhere in New England," I pointed out.

"Oh, yeah!" Shantal laughed. "And they are the only people left on the earth."

"And they have to intermarry to populate the earth." Susie giggled. "They've all been with each other."

"Well, not in the Biblical sense." Lilian rolled her eyes. "You're lucky if you even see a kiss in those movies. Boooring."

"I think they're sweet," Susie said. "They really make you believe in true love."

"So fake!" I rolled my eyes. "The men on Lifetime are more like the men you're going to meet in real life."

"You can say that again." Shantal nodded. "Psycho eyes and cheater faces."

"Oh yeah, I've met so many cheaters in this city." Lilian made a face. "Did I tell you about the guy I went on a date with last month?"

"No." I shook my head. "But hold on. I want to hear, really I do, but let me just message Green Eyes back first."

"You're going to go right?" Susie frowned at me. "We all want you to go."

"Yes, I'll go, but only because I'm curious about him now. Maybe he's not as big of a jerk as I thought he might be."

"Yeah, girl. I bet he's not." Susie sounded so positive that I almost believed that she really knew what she was talking about.

"From your mouth to God's ears." I laughed as I texted him again.

Okay, I can meet you in an hour and a half.

You made my night.

Really?

Learn how to take a compliment.

Okay. Well, thanks.

Meet me at Popsicles. I'll send over the address in a bit.

Sounds good.

"Okay, so I'm meeting him in a little over an hour." I tried to hide my excitement. "So, Lilian, tell us about the guy you went on a date with last month."

"I don't normally kiss and tell, but this one was absolutely crazy." Lilian poured the last of the sangria into my glass and stood up. "I'm going to need another drink before I get into this one. This round's on me."

"I'll help you." Shantal stood up as well. "Plus, I'm feeling like there's a snack at the bar that I want to eat." She nodded towards the bar and we all turned to look. There was a tall man with short black hair and big muscles. He must have sensed us looking at him because he turned towards us and smiled. "Where in the name of Boris Kodjoe did he come from?" Shantal fanned herself. "Do they come much hotter than him?" She twirled her hair and squared her shoulders. "Excuse me, ladies, I spy a man that needs to get my number."

Susie and I watched as they walked to the bar, and my jaw dropped when Shantal walked right up to the hot guy.

"Wow, she's bold." I sipped on my drink. I wanted to be more confident when it came to approaching men. "I wish I could just go up to hot guys like that."

"Me too." Susie leaned back and ran her fingers through her hair before sighing deeply. "I really need to figure out my life."

"What do you mean?"

"Well, you have a new job and new friends, whom I love by the way, but I just feel like I'm doing nothing." She rubbed her forehead with her bright red nails and sat up straight. "I feel like life is passing me by."

"Oh no! Susie, I didn't know you felt that way. Do you want me to stay?"

"Oh, no way!" She shook her head. "You go and meet up with Green Eyes, and when you get home, I'll be waiting up to hear all about it."

FOURTEEN

"And then he said stick this up your ass," Lilian had us all in giggles. "I said why don't you stick it up your own ass. And then he said, "Well, my wife tried to do that to me last night."

"Oh no." I groaned through giggles. "You're right, he sounds awful."

"Then I was like your wife? I thought you said you were divorced? And he was like oh did I? I must have been sleep-walking. Does that even make sense?"

"No," I shook my head and stood up. "As much as I've loved these stories, I have to leave now."

"Good luck, girl." Susie jumped up and gave me a hug. "Have fun."

"You're not leaving us, are you Susie?" Shantal pouted. "I was thinking we could all go dancing."

"I'm so down." Susie grinned and I waved goodbye. I was so happy that my best friend and new friends were getting on; especially now that I knew Susie was feeling left out. I hadn't even realized she was feeling that way, but I was determined to help her find a job and to find love. She deserved everything wonderful that could happen to a person.

I made my way out of the bar and pulled up Google Maps on my phone. I put in "Popsicles" and saw that it was only a twenty-minute walk away. I was feeling happy and buzzed and so decided to save my cab fare and walk to the bar. I sang one of my favorite Passenger songs to myself as I made my way down the New York City streets. There was something so vibrant about the city and I couldn't quite believe that I lived here. I had been dreaming about being in the City my entire life and I was now here.

I got to Popsicles with two minutes to spare. I walked into the bar and looked around. I was surprised to see that the bar was low-key; almost a dive bar. To the right, there were some dartboards and just past that were some table hockey tables. I looked to see if I could locate Green Eyes, but he hadn't yet arrived.

"Looking for me?" A deep voice sounded behind me and I turned around. It was him. All sparkling eyes and gorgeous lips. He really was too handsome for his own good.

"Yeah, something like that." I nodded.

"I wasn't sure you'd actually come."

"Oh?"

"Yeah, I thought maybe you were playing with me."

"Why would I do that?"

"I don't know." He grinned. "You didn't seem too happy to chat with me when we met the other night."

"I changed my mind."

"Good good." He looked around. "So want to buy me a drink?"

"Sorry?" I raised an eyebrow.

"Sorry about what?" He licked his lips. "The bar is over

there." He pointed to the back of the room and started walking.

"You want me to buy you a drink?"

"You're the big shot." He shrugged. "I figured you'd want to."

"Hmmm." I didn't know how to answer that. "What do you want to drink?"

"Well, are we going big or what?"

"What do you mean going big?"

"This is our first date right?"

"Yeah, I guess?" I could see his lips were twitching and I had no idea what game he was playing. "Why?"

"Shouldn't we get something that is memorable?"

"Sorry you're losing me..." I frowned as he grabbed a menu. "Are you going to tell me your name?"

"Let's say Anwir."

"Anwir?" I stared at him. Something in my brain was buzzing, but I didn't know why.

"Yeah." He nodded. "Why don't we get a bottle of Dom?"

"Dom?" My heart started racing. "Like the champagne?"

"Yes, just like the champagne. Maybe when we go to Paris we can visit Champagne."

"When we go to Paris?" I licked my lips nervously. Was Anwir a psycho? Shit, was I in my very own Lifetime movie. What would they call this one? Woman with the Psycho Green Eye Man? Shit, I wanted to make movies; not be the subject of one.

"Don't look so nervous, Marcia." He burst out laughing. "I'm just joking."

"Oh phew."

"We should visit California first. Maybe we can go to Yosemite and Monterey."

"Yeah maybe." I wanted to grab my cellphone and have Susie give me an emergency call.

"You have a corporate card right?"

"Yeah." I wish.

"So just put the trip on that. Maybe we can even fly first class. I've always wanted to fly first class."

"Do you have miles for that?" My voice was sharp now. This man was certifiable.

"Miles?" He laughed. "Do I look like I have miles?" I stared at him then. Really really studied him. He had on nice shoes; nothing fine Italian leather, but nice. His shirt was crisp and cotton. More Kohl's that Brooks Brothers and his watch was more Kmart than Tag Heuer. I looked at the scruff on his face that indicated he hadn't shaved in at least a month. It wasn't crazy and was well kept but he certainly didn't look like the wolf of Wall Street.

"No, you don't. And I don't care if you don't make much money, but that doesn't mean I'm going to spend all my money on you." I licked my lips nervously. Especially seeing as I had $384.23 to my name and that was going to go to my umpteen bills.

"Use that corporate credit card. I'm sure your dad, Finn Winchester won't mind?" He grinned at me and I swallowed hard. My face was growing red and hot. Was this man making fun of me?

"Finn Winchester trusts me and I would never think of betraying his trust. He has a very small circle of loyal friends and I would never do anything to leave that circle."

"Oh yeah?" He looked impressed. "He must really value you."

"Yes, yes he does."

"Call him."

"Excuse me?"

"Call him." His smile dazzled me as he leaned in closer to me. "See if he wants to join us for a drink. I'd love to see him."

"He's not available."

"Oh? Is he too busy tracking people down?"

"What?" I frowned. "What are you talking about?"

"Nothing." He shook his head. "So are we getting this bottle of Dom?"

"No." I pressed my lips together. I was regretting having agreed to this date. Anwir was annoying and obnoxious and it had nothing to do with his looks. "I might actually have to leave."

"Oh, are we going back to your place?"

"What?" My eyes widened.

"I like how you think? Why waste time right?"

"You what?" My jaw dropped.

"We can get down and dirty. Do the damn thing."

"Okay, that's enough. What the hell is your problem?"

"What?" He gave me an innocent look. "Am I supposed to pretend I don't find you sexy as hell?" He looked me up and down. "Like really sexy."

"Well, thanks, but that doesn't mean that we're going to be hooking up."

"I'd like to get my hands all over your fine ass." He licked his lips. "I love a bit of spanking, don't you?"

"What?" I stared at him in shock. "Spanking?"

"Don't worry you can spank me as well!" He winked. "Daddy's been a bad boy."

"Okay, sorry Anwir, but this is not going to work." I shook my head and took a step away from him. This guy was crazy. Granted he was hot as hell, but I wasn't desperate. I didn't need to waste my time with a loser. Even if the thought of his hands on my ass did turn me on a little bit.

"What's not going to work?"

"This." I waved my hands back and forth. "I should have trusted my initial gut instinct, but we're just too opposite."

"Like Romeo and Juliet?"

"What?"

"Like Ken and Barbie?"

"I have no idea what you're talking about."

"Like Kermit the Frog and Miss Piggy?"

"Look dude, I'm not sure if you took drugs or what's going on, but you and me, we're never going to be."

"Well, you never know." He shrugged. "I'm sure we'll see each other again soon, and maybe then you will give me another chance."

"I hope not and I doubt it." I shook my head. "Good bye, Anwir."

"Good bye, sweet butt." He said with a chuckle in his voice and I just turned around and headed out of the bar. I felt like I was in the Twilight zone. What the hell had just gone down? My phone beeped and I pulled it out of my bag.

If you want some no strings attached sex, I'm still down. I stared at the message from Anwir. This guy was too much.

No thanks.

I've been told my tongue is like a power drill.

Is that meant to be a good thing?

Never had any complaints.

Good night. I powered my phone off and headed home. I was tipsy and horny enough to end up typing something back that I would regret.

I MADE my way into the apartment ready to tell everything to Susie, but she wasn't at home. Frustrated, I took off my clothes and got into bed. I powered my phone back on and saw another message from Anwir.

Do you hate me now?

It will be awkward when we next meet.

Sweet dreams, Marcia Lucas.

I stared at the messages and I couldn't stop myself from smiling. Anwir was an idiot, but he had been a hot idiot. I wasn't going to feel bad about the date because I had a brand new job that was looking up and I was determined to make the most of my new position.

FIFTEEN

My heart was racing so fast that I thought I was going to have a heart attack. I stood in the doorway to my new office and squeezed my hands together. My monitor was on and there was a post-it note stuck at the top.

I could read it from where I was standing, but I walked closer to the screen to read it again. I pressed my lips together and held in a scream. The note read, "Got your email. A million years is up. See me in my office. Your boss, The Yeti Finn Winchester.

"Oh shit, oh shit." I pressed down on the mouse and went to my email program. The email I'd drafted the day before was no longer in the draft box. It was in sent mail. "How in the hell?" I swallowed hard and took a couple of deep breaths. I could run out of the office and never look back. I could tell Susie some lie about why I couldn't work there anymore or I could tell her the truth; it was partly her fault after all, for having given me the suggestion.

"Hey, Marcia." Jasper stopped by my door and gave me a quick nod.

"Uh, hi." I swallowed hard. Maybe I could see someone

had played a prank on me? Maybe I'd say Gloria had always had it out for me, but as much as I couldn't stand her, I knew I couldn't lie.

"Mr. Winchester is in today." Jasper smiled. "He'd like to see you in his office."

"Oh?"

"Yes," he nodded. "I assume he wants to welcome you to Winchester Enterprises."

"Does he normally do that?" I squeaked out, my face a deep hot red.

"Sometimes." He said, but his face belied his words. I was going to get fired. This was it.

"Uhm okay. Where is his office?"

"Go up to the top floor. He has the entire floor."

"Of course he does." I laughed and licked my lips nervously. "He wants me to go now?"

"Yeah. I guess so."

"Okay." I headed towards the elevator and pulled out my phone. I saw that I had a text from Anwir. I opened it as I waited for the elevator to arrive.

I thought about your ass all night.

Free tonight?

I stared at his texts and rolled my eyes as I walked into the elevator. What an idiot. I pressed the button to go to the top and wondered what I would say to my new boss. How did I tell the CEO of the company that I only meant to write the email to vent because of his ridiculous demands? Maybe I can say I was pranking him because I thought it was April 1st? No, that was stupid. Too stupid to even mutter out loud. I was dead. The ping of the elevator alerted me to the fact that I'd arrived at my destination. I stepped out of the elevator and walked to the desk that was standing slightly to the left.

"Good morning," An elderly woman smiled at me. "Can I help you?"

"I'm Marcia Lucas, I, uhm, just joined the executive team and was told Mr. Winchester requested to see me."

"Oh sure." The lady pushed the glasses up her nose. "One moment please." She picked up the phone on her desk and pressed a button. "Hello, Mr. Winchester, I have a Marcia Lucas here saying you wanted to see her? Yes, certainly." She placed the phone back down and stood up. "Mr. Winchester said to show you to his office, so this way please." I nodded and followed her down a small hallway; she knocked and then walked away.

"Come in," a deep voice sounded through the door and I swallowed hard. I was so dead. I walked into the office and saw a tall man looking out of the expansive windows. His back was to me and he was wearing a charcoal gray suit. "Ms. Lucas?" The voice was gruff, but yet still he didn't turn.

"Yes, it is I." I licked my lips. "Look, I can explain. I think there's been some sort of misunder..." My words trailed off as he turned around. "You." My jaw dropped as I stared at the handsome face in front of me. It was Green Eyes. "Anwir?" I frowned.

"Liar." He said as he stepped closer to his desk.

"No, I wasn't lying. I was..." I chewed on my lower lip.

"No, that's what Anwir means." He grinned. "It's a Welsh name and it means liar."

"So, your name isn't Anwir?" I blinked, trying to process everything.

"No, it's not." He walked towards me and stopped a mere yard from me. "Surely you recognize me, Marcia?"

"Uhm...." I chewed on my lower lip.

"Aren't you in my close circle? In fact, don't I look at you as a daughter?"

"Well, I didn't exactly say that..." I was starting to hyperventilate. How could this be happening? "Finn?"

"Yup, The Yeti himself." He grinned, his green eyes mocking me. I stared at his face in shock. How did he look so different? He'd lost about twenty years. But then I realized the unkempt beard must have aged him.

"Well, I didn't mean that..."

"What? Cat got your tongue?" He laughed. "Or maybe the cat for your $60,000 corporate credit card?"

"You should have told me." I pointed at him, my face bright red. "You knew all along."

"Well, not when I first said hello. I thought you were a normal woman then." He shrugged. "It didn't take me long to figure out you were just a disgruntled woman with issues who also likes to lie...a lot."

"What was last night about then?" I glared at him.

"I wanted to have a laugh." He chuckled. "I figured two could play the acting game."

"I wasn't an asshole to you though."

"Oh yeah?" He winked. "I mean you did say in your email that I would be so lucky as to see your fine ass...so I was hoping that last night my dreams would come true."

"What would you have done if I would have said yes?" I glared at him. "What if I'd let you come back to my place. Would you have told me?"

"I was fairly certain that wouldn't happen." He shook his head. "The way your eyes were shooting daggers at me. To be honest, I was surprised you even agreed to the drink."

"I knew I should have avoided you." I sighed. "The good looking ones are always drama."

"You can say that again." He crossed his arms and stared

at me with a pointed look. "No one told you to lie and say you were the President of Marketing. Imagine my surprise when my brand new temp was going around telling strangers all about me and my business."

"I mean, I was just..." I paused. There was nothing that I could say that would put this in a positive light. I had definitely messed up. "So am I fired?"

"I don't know yet." He shook his head as he studied my face. "You did take the tests and sign the contracts not to seduce me."

I rolled my eyes as he smirked. So green eyes was Finn Winchester. I just couldn't believe it.

"So you knew?" I glared at him. "You knew it was me and that's why you made me do those ridiculous tests and sign that ridiculous contract?"

"Maybe, maybe not." He ran his hands through his silky dark brown hair. "You seem the sort that would try and have her wicked way with me, so I just had to let you know that I'm off limits." He licked his lips and grinned as my jaw dropped.

"Trust me, I don't want you." I could feel that my entire body was hot and bothered and the devil inside of my hand was calling me a liar. I wanted to tell him off. I wanted to kiss him, then slap him and walk out of the office with my head held high, but I needed the paycheck. I literally needed every cent that was coming. Susie would not be impressed if I was fired now.

"Sure, you don't."

"Why didn't you tell me?"

"Because it was fun listening to you talk." He shrugged. "Plus you're funny. You'd be funnier if you weren't a liar, but still, I enjoyed our interactions."

"You think I'm an idiot, don't you?" I sighed as I stared at him. "You just look so different."

"It's amazing what a good razor, a haircut and some well fitted suits can do for a man."

"I guess so." I nodded, trying not to notice just how well those suits were fitting his body.

"I bet you want me to buy you a drink now though, huh?" He gave me one of his self-assured grins and I remembered why I'd initially thought he was a cocky bastard. "Debating whether or not you can have another chance with me?"

"You can kiss my ass, Finn." The words slipped out of my mouth before I could stop them. Shit, I really wanted to be out on the streets.

"Is that an offer, Marcia?" He raised a solitary eyebrow as he took another step closer to me.

"Is what an offer?" I took a step back.

"Are you asking me to kiss your ass?" His eyes peered at me as if he were asking me the most important question in the world. "Or would you prefer me to bite it?"

"That's...that's not an appropriate question."

"I think you crossed the line of appropriateness a long time ago, Marcia."

"So where do we go from here?" I folded my arms. I was not going to let him intimidate me. Yes, I'd messed up, but I needed to know what was going to happen now.

"You tell me?" He pulled out his phone. "There's a Hilton a few blocks from here."

"A Hilton?" I paused. "The hotel?"

"Bingo!"

"A hotel?" I shook my head. "You think I'm going to go to a hotel with you? You think I'm just going to say, sure Finn, let's go and get down and dirty and..."

"Marcia..." He shook his head. "Did you do any research on my company before applying for a job here."

"Of course I did."

"Well then you would know that I am in talks with Hilton to be one of their suppliers of linens." He stared at me with a stern expression. "I have a meeting today with the general manager of the local Hilton to visit the different suites. I thought perhaps you would want to come and take notes...seeing as you were hired to my executive team."

"Oh." I didn't know what to say. "So I'm not fired?"

"Not yet." His lips twitched. "Though that can be arranged."

"Uhm, that's okay." I brushed my hands down the front of my skirt to smooth it down. "I can go to my office and grab my notebook and a pen and we can get to work right away, Mr. Winchester."

"Not calling me Finn any longer?"

"I don't think that's professional, do you?"

"I don't mind being unprofessional." He grinned.

"Let's get one thing straight Mr. Winchester, I am sorry for exaggerating my position in the company, but I want to make it clear that I'm not interested in flirting or anything else. I am a professional and I hope you will be one as well."

"So you're not attracted to me anymore?"

"Who said I was attracted to you?"

"You came on the date last night."

"It wasn't a date."

"It was a date." He nodded. "Who hurt you?"

"Who hurt me? What are you talking about?"

"You've been defensive since the first time we met. I'm just curious why."

"Maybe I don't trust men that are too good looking for their own good."

"You think I'm too good looking?" He grinned.

"Too good looking, too rich, too cocky, too everything." I nodded. "I'm not interested in anything you're offering."

"But I haven't offered anything yet."

"Well that's good then." I stared at him for a few seconds. "So are we going to go to this hotel or what?"

"Yes." He nodded and turned around. He walked back to the window and looked out. "It's a beautiful city, isn't it?"

"Yes," I said softly. "You have an amazing view."

"It's not the view I want, but it sure is amazing." He turned around and sighed wistfully. I stared at him wondering why he looked so pensive. What did he have to be so sad about? He was literally a billionaire, with a view that millionaires would envy. He had everything going for him. I couldn't even pay my rent. "Meet me down in the lobby in 15 minutes." He said suddenly. "You're dismissed, Marcia."

"Okay, thanks. I'll be there." I walked to the door and exited his office. I felt slightly off, like my world was off-kilter.

SIXTEEN

He was waiting for me in the lobby and as I walked out and towards him, I could feel butterflies in my stomach. I didn't know why. It wasn't like this was a date. In fact, I didn't think that he would ever be interested in asking me out again. And I couldn't blame him, considering the fact that I'd lied to him the very first time I'd met him and I'd signed a contract saying I wouldn't seduce him or do anything with him and I'd called him an asshole.

"Hey there, Marcia." Shantal waved and smiled at me. "What's up?"

"I'm just going to do some work with Mr. Winchester." I nodded my head towards him, and she slapped her hand against her mouth. Finn turned around and looked at me, a smirk on his face as he surveyed me.

"I see you've been getting to know everyone, Marcia. And you've not been here but a couple of days."

"Well, Shantal and I met on my first day, and she's really nice and..."

"Don't tell me. She was one of the girls you were having drinks with yesterday."

"Actually, yeah. How did you know?"

"Because she seems like that sort of woman."

"What does that mean?"

"I mean, it seems like she's the sort of woman that likes to have fun, right?"

"Yeah, and?"

"And what?" He shrugged. "I'm not saying it's a bad thing. I'm saying you're young. You want to have fun in the city. Drinks are fun."

"Okay."

"Everything I say doesn't have a double meaning. You know that, right Marcia?"

"I guess so. I mean, it's just hard to believe when..."

"When what?" he interrupted me. "Remember the first time we met?"

"Vaguely."

"Remember, I was introducing myself. I was friendly. You were the one that lied to me and dismissed me."

"I didn't mean to lie to you, and I was dismissing you because I was having a private conversation with my best friend and..."

"I know, I know. You've been hurt."

"Why do you keep saying that?"

"Because I can see that your walls are up," he said, his eyes peering into mine. It felt like he was looking into my soul and at every heartbreak that had ever broken me.

"Well, it doesn't matter who may or may not have broken my heart. We are not going to have any more conversations about this because we are professionals and..."

"Yes, yes, Miss Lucas. Come on. Let's go."

"That's it?" I said frowning.

"What?" He shrugged, looking at his watch. "We have to be there within 30 minutes, so let's go."

"I mean, we were just having a conversation and..."

"And what? You told me the it wasn't professional and you didn't want to talk about it anymore."

"Yeah, but..."

"You can't have it both ways, Miss Lucas. You can't want to be in my employ and want to be in my bed. I mean, you can if you really want, but we just have to set some ground rules." He grinned. "I'm okay with that if you are."

"No, that is not what I'm talking about," I said flustered, thinking about lying in his bed. "I..."

"You what, Marcia?"

"Nothing." I shook my head. "Let's go."

"And go we shall." We walked out of the front of the building, and I turned around to look at Shantal staring at me, her mouth slightly agape. I wondered just how much of our conversation she'd heard.

"And I do know you're not going to go and tell your friends everything we talked about," he said. "You did sign a confidentiality agreement, and you also signed a nondisclosure agreement."

"In regards to my work, not in regards to my private life."

"I'll find if you read that confidentiality agreement one more time, you'll see that your private life is pretty much tied into that as well, especially when it concerns me."

"You're absolutely ridiculous. What, are you going to sue me if I tell my friend that my boss is green eyes?"

"Green eyes?" He grinned. "So is that the name you gave me?"

"Well, it's certainly not Anwir." I glared at him.

"What? I thought it was quite clever, actually."

"Really?" I said. "Anwir? Liar? What?"

"It took me 30 minutes to come up with that name."

"What do you mean it took you 30 minutes to come up with that name?"

"Well, I knew when you got to the bar you would want to know my name, and of course I couldn't tell you that I was Finn Winchester because you'd run out of there really fast."

"I ran out of there really fast anyways."

"Yeah, but that's because I wanted you to." He grinned.

"You wanted me to run out of there and leave you in the middle of the bar by yourself."

"Okay, maybe I didn't want you to run out. Maybe I was seeing how far I could push you. Maybe I was hoping that perhaps you'd go back with me to my place and you'd shown me that fine ass of yours."

"Really?" I glared at him. "Enough."

"You look like you're mad, Marcia." He laughed. "Or rather, that's your normal expression when you look at me."

"Yes it is, because I think you're totally impertinent and..."

"And what?"

"Nothing," I said. "Are we catching a car to this hotel or..."

"I thought we'd walk."

"Walk?" I groaned slightly as I looked down at my heels. My heels were not made for walking, at all, very long. "Do we have to walk? Because..."

"Because what? You don't like to exercise?"

"I mean, I don't mind walking, but I'm wearing heels. And if we're going to walk to this hotel, I really need to change my shoes."

"What do you mean you need to change your shoes?" He looked confused.

"I have my flats upstairs in the office. I wore my flats to

get to work and then I changed into my heels once I got to the office because they look more professional and..."

"Okay." He stared at me as if I were crazy. "You do know that this is a workplace and..."

"And what? Is there something wrong with me changing from flats to heels?"

"No, but you could've just wore flats in the office. Who are you trying to impress?"

"Oh, I'm just trying to impress everyone in the office." I rolled my eyes. "Maybe I want to impress Japer or maybe I want to impress Sebastian or..."

"I see." He shook his head. "So you're another one going for Sebastian, huh?"

"What do you mean another one going for Sebastian?"

"Almost every woman in the building has either gone for me or Sebastian. And they know they can't get me, so..." He shrugged.

"Oh yeah, because every woman wants you."

"Pretty much." He grinned. "I mean, you heard about the girl that said I knocked her up." He laughed. "I mean, you told me the story when you thought I was someone else."

"So that was true?" I stared at him. "Really?"

"Yep." He nodded. "You can't make that shit up. So," he put his hand up in the air, "we can take the car then."

"Are you sure?" I said. "I mean, I can run up real quick and put my flats on and..."

"No, I like your legs in those heels." He grinned. "We'll take the car." A Lincoln Navigator pulled up, and a man jumped out of the driver's seat and opened the back door for us.

"Hello, Mr. Winchester."

"Hi there, David. This is a new member of the executive team, Marcia. Marcia, this is my driver, David."

"Hi, nice to meet you."

"You too." He nodded. I slid into the backseat and then Finn slid in next to me. David closed the door after Finn slid in.

"Wow, so you have a chauffeur?"

"That surprises you?" He laughed.

"No."

"Then why did you mention it?"

"I don't know. Something to say. We don't all live in the world of the rich and the elite, you know. Some of us actually take the subway and..."

"I take the subway."

"Really? You take the subway?"

"You called me a Yeti." He grinned. "Do you think a Yeti drives around in a chauffeur-driven car all the time?"

"I don't know." I shrugged. "I've never met a Yeti before I met you."

"Why does that not surprise me? So, Marcia."

"Yeah?"

"Have you ever been camping or hiking or rock climbing or..."

"Oh, hell no." I laughed. "Why would I do any of those things?"

"I don't know." He looked disappointed. "Maybe because you enjoy nature?"

"Nature's okay, but hiking is hard, especially when you have to climb mountains and shit. I'm not made for that. I'm from Florida. It's flat in Florida."

"Yeah, but it's not pretty."

"Have you ever been to the beaches? They're gorgeous. St. Pete Beach and Siesta Key and Miami Beach and..."

"I've seen them." He shrugged. "I prefer the mountains myself. And a lake." He looked wistful again. "But it is what it is." I stared at him for a few seconds and thought back to what he'd said in his office earlier.

"Oh, is that it?" I said out loud, staring at him.

"Is what it?" He frowned.

"You don't like the city, do you?"

"What makes you say I don't like the city?" He shook his head.

"You would rather live in the mountains. So you are Yeti. You're like a mountain man, a Neanderthal, a..."

"Not quite, Marcia." He shook his head. His eyes were keen on my face. "You are astute, though. Yeah, I do like the mountains." He nodded. "I always thought I'd end up living in Montana or Colorado or Wyoming. Shit, I'd even live in North California if I had to."

"So then why are you in New York City?"

"Because this is where my company is headquartered and this is where I have to be for now."

"Okay."

"But I try to get away as often as possible. I just love to climb mountains. In another life, maybe I would've opened a cabin somewhere and had a little ski resort."

"You could still do that if you wanted to. I mean..."

"No, it's not possible." He shook his head. "But it is what it is. I enjoy my job. I enjoy making money and I enjoy brokering deals. I guess we can't always have everything in life."

"But if you don't like the city, why live here? I mean, don't you have enough money?"

"What's enough?" he said. "So you really like New York City then, huh?"

"It's amazing. I nodded. "I never really thought I'd live in the city. I grew up in a small town in Florida and, well, it just seemed like a pipe dream, you know? But one day I said to myself, 'I'm going to do it. I'm going to do it for me and my best friend, Susie.' You met her that night at the bar. Well, we moved here together and we've been here a couple of months. And I still pinch myself every morning that I wake up."

"So you're fresh in town." He grinned and nodded. "I guess you grew up watching Sex and the City and shows like that, huh?"

"Maybe. I mean, Carrie's okay, but I wouldn't necessarily want the experience she had."

"I hope not." He laughed.

"You've seen Sex and the City?"

"Some people call me Mr. Big." He winked.

"Oh my gosh. Really, Finn?"

"What? Like the character, though they could be referring to other things as well."

"You're too much. You know that, right Finn Winchester?"

"Yeah, I do." He nodded. "Also, Marcia?"

"Yeah?" I said looking at him, nervously wondering what he was going to say.

"Welcome to Winchester Enterprises."

"Thank you," I said softly. "That means a lot."

"You're welcome," he said. "Now prove to me that I made the right decision keeping you on after I found out what a big liar you are. I really, really don't want to have to fire you next week and then have you storming into my office shouting that I'm an asshole and an ass licker."

"What?" I blinked at him. "What's that supposed to mean?"

He winked and laughed. "You'll see."

SEVENTEEN

All I could think about was a retort in my mind, but I kept my lips shut. I knew he was trying to rile me up. I knew he wanted to get into some sort of back and forth with me, but I wasn't going to let him do it. Though, the image of him licking my ass made me blush. No one had ever licked my ass, and I wasn't sure I ever wanted anyone to do it. I mean, I'd heard that people enjoyed it, but I just couldn't see how. I certainly wasn't interested in licking his ass.

"Cat got your tongue?" he said, and I stared at him.

"No, I was just thinking about something."

"Something good, or..."

"No, I was just thinking about the sort of linens we are hoping to supply to Hilton."

"Oh," he nodded. "Back to work, I guess."

"Well, that's why we're headed there, correct?"

"Correct," he nodded, his lips twitching. "So, can I ask you a question?"

"Sure," I said, "as long as it's not about my ass." I smiled at him sweetly.

"Hmm, don't worry, Marcia, I don't have any questions about your ass today," he laughed.

"Okay, so what's your question then?"

"When you said you were president of marketing, was that because you hoped to be president of marketing and you're really interested in marketing or..."

"Oh, we're going to go back to that again, are we?"

"I'm just curious. I'd like to know where you see your career going."

"Wow. We're talking about career trajectory on my first official date? I don't know if I should be super happy or..."

"Or what? Is there anything other than happy to be?"

"I guess not. Initially I applied for the president of marketing position." I made a face. "And I wasn't qualified, and so my name was not even put forward by the agency," I laughed slightly. "I know, ridiculous, right? But I guess you have to dream big if you want to make it."

"That's a good attitude to have. So, instead you decided to become a temp?"

"Well, it's not like I had much of a choice. The temp agency said to me, "We are not going to put your name forward for the president of marketing because your resume doesn't reflect the skills needed or the work history, but Winchester Enterprises is looking for temps and your degree gets you in the door for that.""

"Okay, so you have no marketing experience or..."

"I mean I have plenty of marketing experience. I am on Facebook. I'm on Instagram. I even started a TikTok account recently, and do you know how hard it is to make yourself look good on TikTok and stand out?

"Tik what?" he said.

"You cannot be kidding me. You've never heard of TikTok?"

"I can't say that I have."

"Have you been living under a rock?"

"No, but I've been in the mountains," he shrugged. "And trust me, no one on Everest was talking about TikTok or snapping selfies."

"No one took a selfie on the top of Mount Everest?"

"Okay," he smirked and then smiled his long drawn out lazy smile, that made me think of Sunday mornings in bed. "Maybe one or two, but that's because it was Mount Everest and we certainly weren't posting it to Instagram immediately."

"Yeah, I get that. Most probably when you got to the hotel, you did though."

"The hotel?" He started laughing. "You really have no clue, do you?"

"I guess there's no hotel on Mount Everest?"

"No, my dear. There's not."

"So anyway," I said, "No, I don't really have any experience marketing for a big corporation or a company. And if I'm 100% honest, I don't really want to be a president of marketing in my life. That's not where I see my life going. I mean, I would love to make the money the president of marketing was going to make, because that would help pay a lot of bills." I realized that I was rambling. I looked at him for a few seconds. "Sorry, I should stop."

"No, it's fine. I like hearing you talk."

"Really?"

"Yeah, really."

"Well, okay then." I really didn't know what to say to that. It was a compliment. I could see it from the way he was smiling at me, but it made me feel uncomfortable. It made me feel like he was seeing me as a woman and not his employee, and the last thing I needed to feel was an attraction to him again. That would make everything far too complicated.

"Anyway, if I'm honest, I actually want to be a documentary filmmaker and that's where I see my career going."

"You want to be a documentary filmmaker at Winchester Enterprises or...?"

"No, I don't want to be a documentary filmmaker at Winchester Enterprises." I rolled my eyes. "Do you even make documentary films?"

"No, but I wasn't sure if you that or..."

"I'm just saying my career goal, where I see myself in 10 years is most probably accepting an Academy Award for a Best Documentary Filmmaker."

"Oh, really? An Academy Award?"

"Well, I mean, I don't know about an Academy Award, but it would be nice."

"And you see yourself still in New York?"

"I don't know," I shrugged. "I mean, I'd like to get married and have kids one day, and I don't know that New York City is the best place to raise kids, especially if you don't have a lot of money, which I don't and..."

"What about your husband? What if he has a lot of money?"

"Knowing my luck, he'll be some broke artist and he won't."

"Oh, so you like artists then?"

I shrugged. I mean I'm open to lots of different guys. I don't really see myself with a Wall Street type. I mean, it would be nice to be wined and dined but..." I paused. "Sorry, you must think I just really ramble on and on."

"No, I think this is the first time you've ever really let me in and actually had a real conversation with me as opposed to just shutting me down."

"I mean I wasn't shutting you down because of you. I just..." I sighed. "You just rubbed me up the wrong way."

"Oh? What was it I did?"

"You're just too good looking and self confident. And I know that sounds absolutely ridiculous, because how can a guy be too good looking and self-confident? But my ex was like you and..."

"Oh, your ex was a handsome billionaire?"

"No," I laughed. "He was broke as hell, but he was very handsome and he played me and he broke my heart and I was a fool, and I told myself I would never let that happen again."

"Ah, so he did break your heart."

"Kind of," I said. "I mean, it was complicated."

"I see. Aren't relationships usually complicated?"

"They don't have to be," I said. "I mean, all my relationships have been complicated and made me feel like shit, but I'm hoping that one day I'll meets someone who doesn't, you know?"

"I know," he said softly. "Sometimes you need to go through the crappy relationships though to really appreciate a good one."

"Wow. Words of wisdom from Finn Winchester. Now I know why you're a billionaire. Is the self-help book coming soon?"

"Maybe," his lips twitched. "If it is, would you help me promote it and market it?"

"I could definitely do that," I grinned back at him.

"Maybe you could even make TikRock video."

"TikTok," I said.

"Isn't that what I said?" He looked at me confused.

"No, you said TikRock. It's TikTok."

"Well, yeah, you can help me make one of them."

"Yeah, sure," I said. "Are we nearly there?"

"Nearly," he said.

"Should we go over the plans or..."

"We don't have to. We'll have more than enough time when we get to the Hilton to discuss business related items. I like getting to know you."

"Why? I'm your employee. I'm..."

"You're unique, Marcia Lucas. You're very, very unique." There was something in the way that he said the words that made me just look at him. The air was fraught with tension and I could feel my heart racing. I stared at his lips, and I could see that he was staring at mine. I wanted him to lean over and kiss me. I wanted to run my hands through his hair and see if it was a silky as it looked. I wanted to taste his lips and see if he was as good a kisser as I thought he would be.

I groaned inwardly. These were not the thoughts that I should be having about my new boss.

"So, Marcia."

"Yeah?"

"Tell me something," he said.

"Sure." I swallowed hard as he shifted his weight and leaned closer to me. This was it. He was going to kiss me. He was going to make me forget my name.

"What are you doing next weekend?" he said softly. I stared at him, not knowing what to say.

"Next weekend?" I mumbled.

"Yeah." He leaned even closer to me. I felt his hand on my thigh and almost closed my eyes. This was it. He was going to kiss me.

"Um, I don't know yet, but..."

"Well, I was thinking," he said softly, his lips coming closer to mine.

"Yeah?" I swallowed hard.

"I was thinking if you're free, then perhaps we..." He ran his fingers up my leg and I licked my lips nervously. This was it.

"I don't know that this is a good idea." I stumbled over my words as I reached my hand up to touch his shoulder. My fingers played with his hair and I leaned forward. My words were not in sequence with my movements, but I didn't care. "What is it, Finn?" I said, as I went to press my lips against his. I shifted my body and put my hand on his thigh, squeezing, feeling his tense muscle, warm and hot underneath me. I ran my hands up his shirt and then my fingers ran across his jawline, waiting, ready. I knew it was a bad idea, but...

"I was just going to say, I have a meeting next week and Northern California, and I was wondering if you would be free to come. We'd have to stay the weekend." His eyes laughed at me as we sat there and I realized I had nearly made a huge fool of myself. He was teasing me, taunting me. He hadn't been about to kiss me, but I knew he had acted like this deliberately. I knew he was trying to get a rise out of me.

"So, what do you say?" he said, licking his lips. Our faces were so close that I could feel his breath against mine, and I suddenly realized I still had my hand on his chest and my other hand in his hair. I sat back abruptly and shook my head.

"I'll have to check." I looked out of the window, my face bright red. I felt embarrassed. I could hear him chuckling next to me.

"You could have done it, you know," he said softly.

"Done what?" I said, turning to look at him.

"You could have kissed me. I know you wanted to. Don't worry, I wouldn't have held it against you. Maybe, just maybe, I wanted it too."

EIGHTEEN

"Mr. Winchester. It's nice to finally meet you. I'm Abigail."
A tall, slinky redhead held out her hand as we entered the
Hilton hotel and I pressed my lips together. It was very
obvious to me that this lady was flirting with Finn and from
the smile on his face; he seemed to realize it as well.

"Hi, Abigail. Great to finally meet you. This is my
assistant, Ms. Lucas."

Oh, so now I was Ms. Lucas. What happened to Marcia
I wanted to glare at him and say something, but I knew that
wasn't professional. "Hello. Nice to meet you, Abigail."

"You too," she said dismissively. "So Finn, I can call you
that, right?" She bat her long eyelashes at him and I rolled
my eyes.

"Of course, Abigail. We're old friends now. We've been
speaking for what? A couple of weeks now."

"Yes, we have. I have to say I really admire the fact that
you are the one that's been in communication with me. So
often I find that executive teams at corporations are the ones
that make these calls, never the CEO."

"I'm a very hands-on type of businessman. I like to think that's why Winchester Enterprises is so successful."

"Well, you certainly are successful," she giggled. "So the plan for the day is we'll start at the penthouse and then we'll go down to some of our executive level suites and then our standard kings and our standard doubles. Sound good?"

"Sounds perfect." He looked at me. "Did you get all that in your notebook, Ms. Lucas?"

"No, should I have?" I stared at him and he shook his head. He looked over at Abigail.

"She's new, so please bear with her."

"What does me being new have to do with me writing down the fact that we're checking out some random rooms?"

"Really, Ms. Lucas?" I chewed on my lower lip and pulled out my notebook and pen.

"I'm good to go, Mr. Winchester. You just let me know what you want me to write down and I'll write it. I studied shorthand in college, so." I stood at him and he looked at me for a couple of seconds. His eyes sparkling.

"Good to hear that. I'm glad to know that you're willing to do whatever I tell you to do."

"That's not exactly what I said."

"Well, now," Abigail said, interrupting us. "Would you like some coffee or some tea, Mr. Winchester?"

"No, I'm fine. Thanks."

"I wouldn't mind," I started in Abigail. Cut me off.

"Oh, also Mr. Winchester, I hope you don't mind, but I have set up lunch for us. I only have a reservation for two though and I can't really change it. Do you think your assistant would be able to make her way back to the office by herself?"

"I'm right here and yeah, I can."

"She'll be fine. I'll just have the driver take her back to the office."

"I can get by myself. I can get there by myself," I said.

"Well, not with those heels, right? Didn't you say your feet hurt when you walked in them for too long?" I pressed my lips together and looked at Abigail. She was smirking.

"Okay, well, this way." She led us down a hallway to what appeared to be a private elevator. "This is the service elevator. Not that the maids and room service to use, but the executives." She smiled. "If you'd like to use the other elevator," she stared at me and I stared back at her. *Was this bitch joking?*

"No, she'll stay with me," Finn said, and I was grateful for one second. If he would've told me to use the other elevator, I would've left the hotel. I would have gone home and never looked back because if he would've thought that was okay, there was no way I would've been able to continue working for him.

"So what exactly are you in need of?" I said staring at Abigail.

"Oh, excuse me, dear?" She said looking at me with a raised eyebrow. "Are you speaking to me?"

"You look like you're the only Abigail in this elevator." I wasn't sure why I was being so snooty. Actually, that was a lie. I didn't like Abigail. I didn't like how she was treating me and I certainly didn't like how she was looking at Finn like she wanted to put her hands all over him and do things to him that no one else should be doing other than me. I almost gasped as I thought of that. "He's not yours, Marcia," I thought to myself. That's when I knew I was in trouble.

"Did you get that?" she said, and I blinked at her. I'd been so focused on the thoughts in my head that I completely tuned her out.

"Sorry, did I get what?" She sighed.

"I know she's new, Finn, but really? This is the sort of help you get these days? I have a couple of executive assistants and if you're in need of one, I would be more than happy to let you borrow one until you found someone a little bit better trained."

"Excuse me?"

"Now, now." Finn hailed his hands up. "Abigail, thank you very much for your offer. This is Ms. Lucas' first day and granted she is a little bit unprofessional, but I'm thinking that her training wasn't adequate and that's most probably the fault of our trainer." I couldn't believe what I was hearing. "But Ms. Lucas," he stared at and gave me a wicked grin, "we are hoping to supply new bed linens, so fitted sheets, cover sheets, pillow cases, shams, duvets, blankets, bathroom rugs, towels, curtains, shower curtains." He paused and looked over Abigail. She flashed him a dazzling smile that made me want to puke. "Is there anything else I'm forgetting, Abigail?"

"No, I think that's all," she said. "As soon as I read about the article in the Forbes magazine about your new sustainable cotton and linen collection, I knew I had to talk to you about outfitting the Hilton hotels that are part of the main chain."

"What does that mean? Aren't all Hilton hotels part of the main chain?"

"Some are franchises," Finn answered.

"Okay. And what does that mean?"

"Franchise hotels are not required to use the same vendors as the hotels that fall under the parent company. You do know what that means, right?" he said.

"Yeah, of course." I stared at him. I had absolutely no idea what he was talking about and I had a feeling he knew it. Today was going to be a long day. We finished the rounds in about three hours and my hand was absolutely aching. I hadn't handwritten so much information since I was in elementary school.

"So Abigail, I actually think that I'm going to have to pass on lunch," he said giving her his best smile. "I think I need to take Ms. Lucas here to lunch and-"

"Oh no, you don't have to do that," I said, shaking my head. "I'm fine. I can grab my own lunch."

"No, I'd like to go over some of the notes with you and discuss your performance today."

"Really?" I said. I could see Abigail glaring at me, and then I smiled. "Actually, that sounds absolutely perfect. Thank you, Finn." He stared at me and started chuckling.

"Well, I'll send some projected numbers to you by the end of the week. Is that okay, Abigail?"

"Perfect. Maybe we can go over them over dinner or something," she said twirling her fingers in her long, red hair.

"Sure," he nodded. "Sounds good."

"When?" she said quickly and I thought to myself, "Wow, she's desperate."

"When?" he said. "Well, I suppose that really depends on when you are available."

"I'm available every night." She cleared her throat quickly. "I mean, I'm not available every night of course. I have dates and other obligations, but for this, I can make myself available because it's very important, you know, and I want us to be able to close this deal as quickly as possible."

"You mean you want to close the deal as quickly as possible."

"Excuse me?" She looked at me.

"I said-"

"Now, now, Marcia." Finn glared at me. "Just let me know and we'll figure something out. Okay, Abigail?"

"Sounds good to me," she beamed.

"Come on, Ms. Lucas," he said. I felt his hand on the small of my back as he guided me down the corridor towards the elevator. We got into the elevator. When it closed, he shook his head. "What was that about?"

"Excuse me? What was what about?"

"Your churlishness and your childishness and...." he growled. "Really?"

"What?" I just stared at him glaring.

"I didn't want this to be the first time, but I guess it will have to be," he said.

"The first time doing what?" I swallowed hard as he stepped towards me in the elevator. He grinned as he put his hand around my waist and pulled me into him.

"The first time for me to kiss you," he said as he pressed his lips down on mine. I sighed blissfully and melted into him as I kissed him back. I moaned slightly as he pulled away from me. "You were very unprofessional today. You do know that, right?"

"I'm sorry, what?" I blinked at him. "You can't just kiss me like that, you-"

"If you're that unprofessional again, I will have to fire you."

"What?" I said almost shouting. "You can't fire me. I just started. I haven't even gotten my first paycheck yet."

"Well, remember that next time you're rude to a potential customer."

"She was..."

"She was what?"

"Nothing," I said, shaking my head.

"What? Were you jealous?" He laughed.

"Jealous of what?"

"Jealous of the fact that she was flirting with me."

"I couldn't care less that she was flirting with you. I just thought you were both unprofessional. I mean, did you see how she was talking to me and treating me?"

"All I saw was two cats who looked like they were ready to fight."

"Are you calling me a cat?"

"Better than a dog, right?"

"Really? I just-"

"You just what?" he said, licking his lips as he looked down at my face. "You want me to kiss you again?"

"No. Really, Finn? I-"

"You what?"

"You shouldn't have done that."

"Don't tell me you didn't like it."

"I didn't."

"Liar," he said.

"Excuse me?" I grinned back at him. "Shouldn't it be Anwir?"

NINETEEN

"I wish you had on appropriate shoes." Finn stared down at my feet and then looked around. His eyes lit up as he spied a shoe store on the corner. "Come on, let's go."

"Go where?"

"To get you some shoes."

"Nuh uh." I shook my head vehemently. "I was lying the other day. I don't have a huge credit line and obviously you know I don't make tons of money. I can't afford to buy any new shoes right now. Susie would absolutely kill me."

"What does Susie have to do with it?" He raised an eyebrow. "And I was going to buy the shoes."

"No, you're not buying me shoes." I said quickly. "And Susie is my best friend and roommate and she's in charge of our finances."

"You guys are really codependent, huh?"

"No, she's just better with managing money."

"I guess I should be thankful we didn't hire you as President of the accounting department."

"Very funny." I glared at him, but I couldn't stop myself from laughing. "So are we going back to the office, or?"

"I thought we could walk and stop for lunch. It's a nice day."

"Oh." I looked down at my heels. There was no way I'd be able to walk more than a few blocks in them. They were already killing me.

"Let me buy you some shoes." He nodded towards the shoe store again.

"No, I'm not owing you a thing."

"Then come with me to San Francisco next week for the conference. And we can call it even."

"I'll still be paid right?"

"Yes, Marcia. Double time, in fact. And we'll put you up in a nice hotel room and you'll get to fly business class with me."

"Are you sure you want me to come?" I raised an eyebrow. "I mean, I'm kind of new and..."

"I want you to come." He grinned. "Spice it up a bit."

"What do you mean by that?"

"Exactly what I said." He winked and then started walking away from me. "Now come on, let's go and get those shoes."

TWENTY

"Well that's not how I expected my first official day of work to go." I walked down the street to the subway station. My mind was still processing everything that I'd found out. Green Eyes was Finn Winchester. The Finn Winchester. And he'd kissed me. I had no idea what it meant. If it meant anything. I was about to walk down the stairs to the subway when my phone started ringing.

"Mama," I smiled into the phone as I answered it.

"Marcia, where have you been? I've been worried."

"I've been at work."

"I haven't heard from you in ages. I was scared you were dead."

"It's been two days, mom." I rolled my eyes. "I'm fine."

"How's the job?"

"Interesting, but good. I might be going to California on a work trip next week."

"California?" My mother sounded dismayed. "You're traveling for work? I thought you were a temp."

"I am a temp. I'm going as an assistant."

"I don't like this, Marcia. What will I tell your father?"

"What do you mean, mom? I'm not running off to California to become an adult actress or anything—."

"What did you say?" My mother gasped. She was far more melodramatic than I could ever be.

"I said I'm not headed to California to make an adult film..." I giggled slightly. I could just imagine my mom's face.

"Marcia, that is not funny. I think you need to come back home. The city has already changed you."

"Changed me how?" I didn't have the patience for a long lecture from my mother. My mother could have been a talk show host; that's how much she loved to hear the sound of her own voice.

"You're talking back and..." I could tell that she was working herself up and I sighed.

"Momma, I'm fine. The job is good. Susie and I are leading boring respectable lives. Do not worry."

"Your father and I want to see you."

"I'm coming home for Christmas...as long as I can get off work."

"See! You're putting your job before us already."

"Oh momma, really?" I sighed. "I will do my best to come home."

"It would be nice if you had a nice young man with you as well. Your dad and I would love some grandbabies."

"Momma!"

"What, Marcia? I'm just saying. I'm not getting any younger."

"I love you, mom, but I have to go."

"Send me photos from California and tell Susie I send my love."

"Will do. Bye momma."

"Bye darling."

I hung up the phone and shook my head. I loved my mom, but sometimes she took every ounce of patience I had and completely drained me. I was about to finally head down to the subway, when my phone rung again. It was Finn. Why was he calling me?

"Hello?"

"It's Green Eyes."

"Hello, Anwir."

"Hello, Marcia, President of marketing." He chuckled.

"What do you want?"

"Is that any way to talk to your new boss?"

"I'm not on the job right now, right? I can talk to you as I wish."

"What are you doing?"

"I'm about to catch the subway and go home and hang out with my best friend."

"Susie?"

"Yes, you remember her name?"

"I do." He paused. "So I'm guessing I can't convince you to join me for dinner."

"Nope. Sorry." I wanted to ask him why he wanted to invite me in the first place, but a part of me was scared of his answer.

"Can I convince you to have me over?"

"Over where?" I blinked. Did he really want to come over to my apartment? Why?

"To your place."

"I don't think so." I shook my head.

"You really have your walls up, don't you?"

"No," I lied. "I just think it's highly inappropriate to have you to my place for dinner. I mean, what if I try and seduce you? I did sign a contract you know?"

"True, you might not be able to resist putting your hands on me."

"Totally, I'm growing hot right now, just thinking about it."

"Oh yeah?" He growled and I grinned.

"Yeah, if I'm not careful, I won't be able to resist unbuttoning your shirt and then your pants...and well, we both know what happens after that."

"You're a tease." His voice was husky now. "You're not a sweet innocent woman are you?"

"Did I say I was?"

"No, but—."

"I have to go, Finn." I cut him off. I was very close to crossing the line. "I don't want to miss the train, the next one won't come for 20 minutes."

"I can pick you up."

"No thanks."

"Meet me for dinner."

"You're my boss."

"Your asshole boss." He laughed.

"Yup."

"So make me pay..."

"What does that mean?"

"I think you know, Marcia."

"I'm going now." I took a deep breath. "Good bye, Mr. Winchester." And then I hung up and ran down the stairs. I felt hot and flustered and confused. I was playing with fire, teasing him like I had. And I knew that out of the two of us, I would be the only one that got burned if we got involved in any capacity that wasn't work related.

TWENTY-ONE

"Good morning, Shantal." I beamed as I walked up to the reception desk. "How's it going?"

"Not bad." She yawned. "Late night!"

"Ooh? Did you have a date?"

"Nope, but I was chatting with one guy on a dating app." She rolled her eyes.

"Oh? Good or bad?"

"It started really great until he asked me if I liked riding."

"Riding?" I questioned her. "Like horses?"

"If the photo of his cock was a horse, then yeah." She grinned. "And don't get me wrong, some guys have beautiful penises. This man did not."

"Oh no. So you shut him down after that?"

"Oh hell no." She laughed. "I got a free pizza out of it."

"You what?" I stared at her in amazement. "Do tell."

"He wanted to have phone sex." She grinned as she lowered her voice to a sultry tone.

"And you told him no?"

"I told him I was hungry and didn't have the energy for phonesex unless I ate."

"Oh," I laughed. "Then what happened?"

"He sent me a gift card code to Doordash." She started laughing. "And I ordered me a large pizza and wings."

"And then you had phone sex?"

"Uhm, not really."

"What do you mean not really?"

"I called him and played Real Housewives of Atlanta on my laptop, while I had a bath and read a romance book."

"Oh Shantal, that's awful."

"Well, you know." She shrugged and giggled. "Serves him right for sending me an unsolicited dick pic."

"Guys are so ridiculous." I shook my head. "Every guy thinks that just because he has a cock, he's a God. Like no dude, you don't have the nicest cock in the world. Have you shaved it? Are you groomed? Do you bathe frequently? Like if you want to be Cock King, at least have a nice one." It was then that I realized Shantal was staring at me with wide eyes and pressed lips. I swallowed hard and turned slowly to look behind me. If Gloria were standing there I would just die. But no, my luck was even worse. My face went bright red as I saw Finn standing there. I wanted a sinkhole to open up right then and there and swallow me whole.

"Hello, Ms. Lucas, passing on important business information again this morning?" His eyes mocked me and I just stared at him. "Do you make it a habit of putting your foot in your mouth or are you auditioning for some reality TV show that I don't know about?"

"Uhm..." I licked my lips nervously. I didn't dare say anything rude in front of Shantal. I hadn't told any of my friends yet that Green Eyes was Finn. I knew that they would think it was hilarious, but I was still processing everything.

"Cat got your tongue?"

"No, but I'm sure he wants to bite down on yours...real hard." I glared at him and I heard Shantal gasping. She most probably thought I was about to get fired.

"Come with me please, Ms. Lucas." Finn pressed his lips together and walked away from the desk.

"Fuck it, I'm dead." I made a face at Shantal and followed behind him. He walked towards the elevators and then stopped to look at me.

"For your information, I'm well groomed." His eyes gleamed at me and I could tell he was laughing and making fun of me. "I could be your very own Cock King, if you want?"

"No, I don't want. Thank you very much." I blushed and shook my head. My mind immediately went to thoughts of his member. I wondered how big he was. He was too cocky to have a micro penis. Though, maybe he was the sort of guy that worked out and got buff to compensate for his average size penis. Though, I didn't know why I was thinking about his penis. I had absolutely no interest.

"So, Marcia..." He grinned at me.

"I do not care about your penis size, Finn."

"Sorry what?" His lips twitched again and I realized what I'd said out loud. He really made me lose my head. I felt like I was 15 when I was around him. All gangly legs, braces, and frizzy hair.

"I didn't mean to say that."

"Uh huh." He nodded. "You just want to..." His voice drifted off as his phone started ringing. I recognized the tune as Young Thugs, "Best Friend." I stared at him in surprise. I never would have believed that clean-cut Finn was into rap. "Finn here, Justin are you okay?" He frowned and I stared at him curious about who he was talking to. "Where are you?" He looked at his watch and sighed. "Okay, stay there, I'll be there in 30 minutes. Do not leave, okay." He turned his phone off and blinked as he looked at my face, as if he'd forgotten I was there.

"Is everything okay?" All of a sudden I felt nervous and worried.

"Yeah, I hope so." He texted something into his phone. "I'm going to have to miss all of my morning appointments."

"Shall I cancel them for you?"

"You?" He snorted. "No, I have a secretary that will take care of that."

"No need to look at me like I just asked if you would give me ten million dollars to start my snail farm business or something."

"Snail farm?"

"I don't want to start a snail farm, it was just an example."

"Certainly." He nodded. "Well, I have to go now."

"Do you want me to come with you?" I wasn't even sure why I'd asked. Of course he wouldn't want me to come with him. His phone call had sounded private and I certainly didn't want to intrude.

"Actually yes." He nodded slowly. "I think you could be helpful."

"Oh really?" I stared at him in surprise. "How so?"

"I think my friend Justin would be more interested in chatting to a pretty woman than to me right now." He shrugged.

"Is this some sort of hookup?"

"Is that all you think about Marcia?" He studied my face. "Did you come to the City with the sole intention of finding different men to hook up with?" He paused. "I don't think so...you wouldn't have blown me off that night if you had."

"Maybe I blew you off because I wasn't interested."

"But we both know that wasn't the case." His face was thoughtful. "You intrigue me."

"Why?"

"Because you're the first woman I've met in a long time who has put me in my place." He grinned. "And you make me smile."

"I do?"

"Surprisingly, you do." He nodded towards the entrance. "Ready to go?"

"Do I need to tell Gloria or Jasper or anyone?"

"No." He shook his head. "I've taken care of it." We walked towards the front of the building and I could see Shantal gawking at me. I was going to have to tell my friends later exactly what was going on. They would never believe me; I didn't even know if I really believed it myself.

TWENTY-TWO

"So I'm glad to see you're not wearing your heels today." Finn looked at my feet as we made our way out of the office building.

I looked at him in surprise. "Oh, we're walking."

"Yeah," he nodded. "That's not going to be a problem, is it?"

"No," I said, "I'm just surprised we're not taking a car. You seem to love to be driven by your chauffeur."

"That's not true at all," he said, shaking his head. "In fact, I very much hate being driven by a chauffer."

There was a light in his eyes that I didn't quite understand, and I stared at him for a few seconds. "Really? Why?"

"This is the life I was born into, not the life that I wanted. It's my responsibility to carry on the family business," he shrugged.

"You didn't want to," I said, finally understanding.

"No, I didn't. I always thought my older brother would take over the company, but..." He paused and signed. "Anyway, it doesn't matter now. What's to be will be and what's not to be won't be."

"You wish you could live in the mountains."

"Yeah," he said. "I'd do anything to live in the mountains."

"But what would you do there?"

"I think I told you I'd open a small little resort."

"Wow. That sounds..." I paused. I didn't want to lie. I didn't think it sounded cool. I mean, it sounded cool, like cold, but it didn't sound cool like fun and exciting. It totally wasn't my thing.

HE started laughing. "I can tell exactly what you're thinking."

"What do you mean?" I said quickly.

"Your face. You know there's a saying that faces are the windows to the soul?"

"I think the saying is eyes are the window to the soul."

And he paused you're right. "I think that's the saying. Anyway, when I look at your face and into your eyes, I can tell exactly what you're thinking. You can't lie."

"Well, I can lie, but-"

"But you can't lie about your emotions," he said. "I can tell when you're happy. I can tell when you're sad. I can tell when you're angry."

"Oh, wow. I didn't know you'd seen so many different emotions on my face."

"Yeah," he said, "I have. So now you know my dream. Tell me more about yours."

"I want to make documentaries. That's why I came to the city."

Oh. Just random documentaries, or..."

"No, I want to tell the stories of Puerto Ricans."

"Puerto Ricans? That's quite specific," he said looking taken aback. "Why Puerto Ricans?"

"Because my mom is from Puerto Rico, and I have a

whole family from Puerto Rico, and I want to get to know more about that part of my background."

"You don't know much about it?" he said.

"Not really," I sighed. "My mum married my dad when they were quite young, and he's Irish American. And I know a lot about that part of my family, and they're lovely. Really lovely. But I don't really know much about my Puerto Rican side, and I kind of wanted to do a documentary on what it meant to be Puerto Rican and American."

"Well, Puerto Ricans are Americans, right?"

"Of course. They are Americans, but they also have their own identity as Puerto Rican. You know? I just wanted to delve into that more."

"So do you speak Spanish?"

"No," I shook my head regretfully. "I wish my mother would've taught me when I was younger. She speaks fluent Spanish, but I guess she didn't think it was necessary." I half laughed. "Little did she know that Spanish would take over the world."

"Yeah, you could have really made it into a high executive position if you were fluent in Spanish," he said with a smile.

"Yeah, but I don't really want to be an executive, no matter what I said about being president of marketing."

"Okay then. So, I guess I won't offer you that position."

I started laughing. "We both know you weren't about to offer me any president position."

"Well, we don't know that for sure, but ..." He nodded. "Most probably not anytime soon."

"Yeah," I said as we continued walking down the street. "I just want to be in the street with my camera and documenting people."

"People or Puerto Ricans?" he asked.

"People. I want to go to the Bronx, and I just want to talk to people, you know? I want to get to know the melting pot of cultures and how it makes up one of the greatest cities in the world."

"You sound like you're really passionate about it."

"I am," I nodded.

"And so how's the documentary going?"

"Honestly, it's not." I shook my head. "I don't have microphones. My camera's kind of old. I don't really know anyone else that's interested in documentary filmmaking." I chewed on my lower lip. "I guess I'm kind of nowhere. It's a pipe dream."

"It's not a pipe dream," he said. "Are you doing anything to get yourself in a position to start making your documentary?"

"Yeah," I said. "This job for one."

"Oh?" He looked surprised. "I thought this job was more about you paying your rent, but..."

"No, it's about paying rent, of course." I heaved a deep sigh. "I feel really guilty."

"Why do you feel guilty?"

"I dragged my best friend, Susie, with me. I had a bad situation back home, and, well, I'd always wanted to move here, and I convinced her to come with me, and she spent a lot of her savings helping to pay the bills for both of us. I know earlier you made a comment asking if we were codependent, and it's not that we're codependent. It's just that I'm not good with money, or rather I don't really have much money. And so that's why it was really important for me to get this job. That's why it was really important for me to be able to provide and pay for the bills that are stressing Susie out day and night. She's my best friend, and yeah, I could get some part-time job and go and buy equipment and start making my documentaries, but that wouldn't be fair to her."

"Does she have a job?"

"Um, not really."

"What do you mean? She either has a job or she doesn't."

"I think she got some like marketing job. That's not really what she wants to do," I sighed. "I feel selfish, you know?"

"Why do you feel selfish, Marcia?"

"I feel selfish because I've always kind of looked out for myself number one. Don't get me wrong, I love Susie, and I would do anything for her, but she's more quiet and she's more compassionate and understanding, and she allows me to pursue my dreams and go for what I want, and she sort of stands back in the shadows. And while I thought she didn't mind, I thought she didn't have dreams of her own, but I'm starting to think that perhaps I was wrong."

"Oh? Why is that?"

"Just a comment she made to me the other day." I shook my head. "I don't think she's enjoying the city as much as I am. Well, at least I don't know," I said. "Are we nearly there?"

"We're about 10 blocks away," he said. "You know, if she really wants a job, she can come and work at Winchester Enterprises. We're always looking for temps."

"Well, I asked Gloria, and..."

"Okay. It doesn't matter what Gloria said if I'm telling you I can hire her."

I smiled at him. "I guess you're pulling rank over Gloria, huh?"

"I am the CEO of Winchester Enterprises. I am Finn Winchester," he grinned.

"Thank you. That's really sweet of you, and you don't even know Susie."

"I know she's your best friend, and I know that she's loyal," he grinned, "and those are two very positive traits. I think she'd make a great addition to the accounting department seeing as she seems to do your personal finances, even if you don't seem to have much."

"Yeah, we don't," I laughed. "But that's no fault of hers. It's my fault, and..." I sighed. "You know, I want to tell you something."

"And what's that?"

"You were kind of right when you said to me I was closed off and was sort of taking stuff out on you when I first met you."

"Oh? How so?"

"So the last guy I dated in Florida, he was gorgeous, and I really fell for him, and he ended up cheating on me. And like a fool, I took him back, and he ended up cheating on me again, and he gaslighted me. He made me feel like it was all my fault, and he made me feel like I was an idiot for expecting that we were in a monogamous relationship and that he had feelings as deep for me as I had for him. It really played with my head."

"I'm sorry. I'm not your ex though. I don't know why you would judge all men based off of one man."

"It's not just about that relationship though." I sighed.

"Oh? What else is it about?"

"When I was in college my freshman year, I dated a man," I groaned. "I don't even know why I'm telling you this, but I felt you should know."

"Tell me, please."

"He was gorgeous, and he was confident and he had money."

"This is a guy in college?"

"No," I shook my head. "I was in college, but he was working already."

"Okay, so he was an older guy?"

"Yeah, and I fell in love with him." I chewed on my lower lip. "Like, I thought we were going to get married."

"Oh, wow. Okay. What happened?"

"Well, one day he told me to meet him for dinner, and I got ready and I waited for him to come and pick me up, and he never came. And so I started getting really worried and was calling him, and he wasn't calling me back, and I even ended up calling the police to see if there'd been any accidents."

"Oh, shit. Was he okay?"

I nodded. "Yeah, he was fine."

"So what happened?"

I played with my hair for a few seconds and then looked at him. "I went out later that evening to get ice cream with one of my roommates and her boyfriend."

"Okay."

"And we drove maybe a couple of blocks away. Not far."

"Okay."

"And I saw his truck. He drove this souped up truck. He used to, like, race them and have them in shows. It was pretty obvious to me that it was his truck."

"Okay. And so he was okay?"

"Yeah, he was more than okay." I rolled my eyes. "His truck was parked outside a sorority house, so I had my friend's boyfriend stop his car, and me and my friend got out. We walked up to the door, knocked, and one of the sorority girls opened, and I said that I was there to see Ricky."

"Oh, boy," he said. "What happened?"

"Well, the girl opened the door and we were walked inside, and I went upstairs, and..." I shook my head. "There was Ricky."

"Oh?" Finn stared at me. "Do you have detailed information, or..."

"He was going down on one of the girls at the top of the stairs, whilst another girl was blowing him."

"No way," Finn said, his eyes wide. "I'm sorry."

"It's okay. I later figured out that he preyed on college girls, and there were a number of us he was fucking with," I sighed. "I had to go and get STD tests just to make sure that he hadn't given me anything, and I just remember feeling like such a fool. And the worst part was he showed up at my door about a month later thinking I was going to take him back, and I can just remember the smug, cocky look on his face, how self-assured and confident he was."

"So that's why you hate handsome and men, because you've been burned?"

"It's not just that I hate handsome men. It's that I just feel like if a man is too handsome and too confident and too cocky and sure of himself, well, it just reminds me of my exes and how they broke my heart and stepped all over me, and it's just hard, you know?"

"I guess I should take that positively," he said with a raised eyebrow. "You think I'm very handsome, but then you're also saying you think I'm cocky and self-assured."

"Come on now, Finn. You're not confident?"

"I don't know," he shrugged. "Maybe I appear to be more confident than I am. Maybe you can't judge a book by its cover."

"You know, you're the second person that's said that to me in the last couple of weeks. Maybe you're right."

"Maybe I am," he said, and then stopped outside a diner. "Okay. We're here."

"Oh, and where is it that we're going?"

"Inside there," he nodded at the diner. "We're going to see Justin."

"Your friend?"

"Yeah. He's my friend, my little brother."

"Oh, I didn't realize you had a little brother."

"Come on. You'll see." He opened the door and looked around and then headed towards the back of the diner. Sitting in one of the booths was a young boy, about 12 years old. "Hey, Justin," Finn said.

The little boy looked up. "Hey, Finn. What's up?"

I stared at Finn, and then I stared at the little boy, who appeared to be Black. I wasn't a scientist or a biologist, but they didn't look like they were related.

Finn nodded towards me. "Justin, this is Marcia."

"Hi," I said. "Nice to meet you."

"Hey. Are you Finn's girlfriend?"

"No, no," I said quickly. "I just work for him at the office."

"Oh, okay," he grinned at me. "I was about to say, Finn, you never told me you had a girlfriend."

"I don't have to tell you everything about my life, Justin." Finn slid into the booth, and I slid in next to him. "So did you get something to eat?"

"Ordered some pancakes," Justin nodded. "And some eggs. "You want anything?"

"Maybe I'll have some pancakes as well. You want anything Marcia?"

I shook my head, confused about the situation I now found myself in. "So you two are brothers?" I hated the fact that I'd asked, but I just really wanted to know.

"Yeah," Justin nodded and grinned. "You think we don't look alike, huh?"

"No, I mean, I would never say that." My face was bright red.

"We don't look alike," Justin laughed. "He's my big brother."

"Um, okay." I looked at Finn, and Finn grinned.

"We're part of the Big Brothers, Big Sister program. Justin's been my little brother for the last four years now, so it's like we're practically blood."

"Practically," Justin said and sat back. "I don't want to go back to school today."

"You know you're going to have to go Justin," Finn sighed. "You can't skip school, and I'm sure everyone must be wondering where you are, and-"

"No one cares about me," Justin shook his head. "Mom's at work, and her stupid boyfriend's just at home, and he don't care."

Finn sighed. "Well, I care, and you need to get your education, especially if you're going to come and work for me."

"I don't need school. School sucks, Justin said. He stared at me. "What do you think, miss?"

"Well, if I'm honest," I said softly, "I didn't really like school either, but I had to go to school in order to go to college, and I had to go to college in order to get a job. I had to get a job so I could pay my bills and achieve my dreams, which is what I'm working on now. So," I said, "even though I didn't like school, it's still helpful. Kind of like spinach."

"Spinach?" Justin looked at me confused. "What do you mean?"

"Well, you know how Popeye had to eat its spinach to be all strong?"

"Uh, Popeye the cartoon?" He looked at Finn.

Finn nodded and laughed. "Yes, Justin, Popeye the cartoon."

"Yeah. Um, do you guys still watch Popeye these days? Sorry. I don't really know any kids."

"Um, I've seen Popeye a long time ago," Justin said, and I wanted to laugh because he was so young as it was. How long could a long time ago have been?

"But Popeye had to eat his spinach," I continued, "to stay strong, even though spinach doesn't even taste that great, and that's kind of like going to school." I groaned. "Okay, that's kind of a shitty metaphor." I slapped my hand against my mouth. "Oh my gosh, I'm so sorry. I-"

"It's fine," Finn chuckled, staring at me. "He's heard worse words than that."

"I have, truly," Justin said with a grin. "Don't worry about it."

"Thanks. Sorry. Like I said, I haven't been around many kids."

"That's okay," Justin beamed at me. "You're cool. I like you."

"Thanks. You're cool too."

"So I guess I will go back to school after my pancakes," Justin said. "But only if..."

"What do you want?" Finn said.

"If we can play basketball this weekend."

"Okay," Finn nodded. "You're on."

"But..."

"Oh, boy. What is it?"

"The lady got to come with us too."

"Who, me?" I said, looking at him in surprise.

"Yeah. Will you come too please, Miss Marcia? I think it'll be fun."

"I mean, if you really want me to," I said softly.

"I do."

I looked at Finn to make sure that it would be okay. "What do you think?"

"I think it sounds like a really great idea," he said. "A really, really great idea."

TWENTY-THREE

Finn and I stood outside the school gates and I wondered what he was thinking. This was a side of him that I'd never even considered. The soft sweet side. The caring side. Though, it wasn't like I knew him well enough to be surprised. Maybe his entire being was one of light and compassion. Maybe he went around the city taking care of old women, stray dogs, and little kids that needed father figures.

"You can stop looking at me like that." He stared at me and smiled.

"Like what?" I blinked at him, confused.

"Like I'm Superman. I'm not Superman or Batman or any sort of savior or superhero."

"I never said you were."

"Your lips didn't, but your face did."

"I just think that it's really cool that you're a big brother to Justin and that you're obviously quite involved in his life."

"How do you know that?"

"The headmistress knew you by name." I grinned. "And so did Justin's classmates."

"He's a good kid." He shrugged. "I'm trying to make a difference..." He paused. "Don't get me wrong, I'm not a soft touch...but Justin is special."

"You met him through the program?"

"No actually." He shook his head and I waited for him to finish.

"Are you going to tell me or what?"

"His mom worked for me." He stared at me for a few seconds. "She was in the accounting department."

"Oh wow. And she doesn't work there anymore?"

"No." He shook his head, but didn't elaborate. "I hang out with Justin once or twice a week. He's a little genius. And he knows he can call on me whenever he wants for anything he wants."

"That's awesome." I tapped my fingers against my leg. "You're a good guy."

"I like to think so." He grinned. "So I was thinking you could have the rest of the day off."

"Really? Why?"

"Because you've been really helpful and I know that this isn't in your job description."

"Many things aren't in my job description." I stared at him and then looked at the cars driving by in the street. I felt like I was having my New York moment. I was standing in a cute dress on a street corner with a handsome man and yellow New York cabs were driving by and beeping. "Are you going to play hooky as well?" I tilted my head to the side and studied his face. A lazy smile crossed his face as he stared down at me.

"Got a better plan for me than work?"

"Maybe." I wasn't sure what plan, but I would come up with one if he wanted me to.

"I canceled my plans for the morning and I really should work this afternoon, but if you want to make it worth my while?"

"I don't know if I can do that..." I shrugged lazily. "You should go back to work. I think I'm going to go and get myself a cupcake and—."

"So you don't want me to come?" He looked so disappointed that I laughed.

"I don't know. It seems like you didn't want to come. I don't want to stop you from making your billions."

"Maybe I want you to."

"So then show me New York..." I bat my eyelashes at him. I was officially flirting with Finn Winchester, billionaire, handsome scoundrel, and most importantly my boss. I wasn't sure what I was doing. Maybe I was out of my mind. Maybe I was finally stepping out of my comfort zone and not letting past hurts stop me.

"So this is turning from you showing me a good time to me showing you a good one?"

"Unless you don't want to."

"I've wanted to since the first time I saw you, Marcia Lucas." His voice was gruff and his eyes were penetrating as we stood there. "I just want to make sure that you really want to or if you're going to bite my head off."

"I'm not going to bite your head off."

"Even if I become the most ridiculously handsome man you've ever seen in your life?" He chuckled and I laughed harder than I had in a long time.

"You're so full of yourself, Finn Winchester."

"Perhaps, but I just want you to give me a chance for me. Don't judge me based on those other bastards."

"I won't, but..."

"But what?"

"The contract I signed? I don't want to get in trouble."

"We'll worry about that when we get to the point where you want to seduce me."

"Maybe I want to seduce you right now."

"Do you?" He grabbed my hand and ran his finger across my palm. "Do you really want to seduce me or are you saying that because that's what you think I want to hear? Because while I would love for you to seduce me. This is not about that. This is about me getting to know you and you getting to know me. This is about us making magic."

"Why do you want to make magic with me?"

"Because one night, I saw this beautiful woman walking into a bar with a friend and I was lucky enough that she stopped next to me. And all I wanted to do was make her laugh and smile. But when I spoke to her, she didn't have the time of day for me." He grinned. "In fact, I annoyed her."

"Well, just a little bit." I grinned.

"Well, I haven't forgotten that moment." His finger ran up to my wrist and he pressed his thumb against my vein. "I want you to experience the magic of a moment with me, just like I experienced with you."

"This could be my first magic New York moment."

"I'd love to be your first."

"I don't know what to think when I'm with you, Finn. I don't know if you're just telling me what you think I want to hear to get into my pants or if you're the sort of man that exists in movies."

"I guess you'll just have to see." He stepped in closer to

me. "But we only have one life and sometimes we have to live each day as if it were our last."

"Is that your mountain man philosophy?"

"Don't underestimate mountain men. When we go to San Francisco next week, will you go camping in the mountains with me?"

"I don't know." I wrinkled my nose. "I'm not a nature girl."

"What if today, we do what you want and next week, we do what I want."

"Uhm, I guess, but aren't we going for work?"

"We can spend the weekend in the mountains before we have to go back to the city and sit in stuffy offices."

"Fine," I said. "I'll give you a chance, Finn Winchester."

"That's all I can ask for." He laughed then and I narrowed my eyes.

"What's so funny?"

"You said never in a million years, but I have a feeling it will be a lot shorter than that."

"We'll see." I shook my head and laughed. Though he was right. I hadn't felt so alive and happy in my life. There were a lot of things I was unsure of, but I was pretty confident that I'd be getting to know my new boss more intimately very soon.

TWENTY-FOUR

"What are you doing home already?" Susie looked up at me in surprise as I burst into the apartment.

"Finn sent me home to change." I was breathless as I started pulling my clothes off.

"You're calling him Finn?" She raised an eyebrow and put the iPad down on the couch. "Isn't Finn your boss and the CEO?"

"Yes, yes, he is." I nodded as I ran my fingers through my hair. "And he's taking me on a scavenger hunt."

"What?" Susie looked confused. "You and all the other new hires or just you?"

"Just me." I said as I looked in my closet for my favorite jeans.

"Hold up a second, Marcia." Susie headed over to me. "What am I missing here?"

"Oh." I bit down on my lower lip and turned around to look at her. "I forgot you didn't know."

"Know what?"

"Ugh, hold on, let me get my phone."

"For what?"

"You'll see." I called Lilian and Shantal and then pressed speaker. "Hey guys, you there?"

"Yes." Lilian responded. "What's going on?"

"I hope you are all sitting down and paying attention."

"You're scaring me." Shantal said. "What happened?"

"So there's something I need to tell you all." I took a deep breath. "I found out Green Eyes real name."

"Oh my gosh, don't tell me that he's Jason Momoa." Shantal screeched. "I will literally scream."

"He's not Aquaman." Susie laughed. "You forgot I was there when she first met him."

"Oh yeah." Shantal sounded disappointed.

"Green Eyes is Finn."

"Finn who?" Lilian said, confused.

"Finn Finn." I said grinning at a shocked Susie.

"Finn fucking CEO Winchester?" Shantal gasped. "Oh Lord, I think I'm having a heart attack. Your asshole from the bar is our boss?"

"Yes." I laughed. "And he's not as bad as I thought."

"Oh Lord no, don't do it, don't do it." Shantal cried into the phone. "That man is a heartbreaker."

"And a dream maker." Lilian giggled. "He is a hottie."

"Marcia, this is not a good idea." Susie looked at me nervously. "You can't be playing around with your boss. It's not going to end well."

"It'll be fine." I cleared my throat. "In fact, we're going to explore the city together."

"Explore what city?" Shantal asked. "Not New York? Girl, aren't you meant to be at work?"

"He gave me the rest of the day off."

"Wow, must be nice." Lilian sounded jealous and I wondered if I'd made a mistake by letting them all know. Maybe I should have kept it to myself for a little while. It wasn't like Finn and I had anything going yet. Though he had kissed me. And he'd said he wanted me to feel magic; though I wasn't really sure what that meant.

"What's that supposed to mean?" I said, feeling a little bit off. I'd been so happy when I'd come into the house to change, but now that I told my friends that Finn was green eyes, I didn't feel like I had their support.

"I'm just joking, girl," Lilian started laughing. "You know how I feel about Finn Winchester. He's absolutely gorgeous. And if I were you, I'd be banging him all day and all night long."

"Oh my gosh, really, Lillian," I started laughing.

"I agree," Shantal said. "I had a feeling you guys had chemistry."

"What are you talking about?"

"When I saw you two today, I felt like fireworks were going off in the lobby. I wasn't sure if I was going to have to call 911 and send for the fire engine."

"You're so dramatic. That is such a lie."

"No girl, I could see that there was something between you."

I looked at Susie and wondered what she was thinking.

"Well, you know I told you to give the guy a chance, and that was before I knew he was Finn Winchester, soon as he smiled. I mean, I don't necessarily want you to lose your job if this doesn't work out, but I want you to go for it. You deserve a shot at love and you deserve happiness."

"Whoa, whoa, whoa. Who said anything about love? We're just going to get some cupcakes and hang out at Central Park."

"Finn Winchester getting cupcakes and hanging out at Central park?" Lillian sounded shocked. "Are you joking? That does not sound like the man I've read about."

"Why? What's the man you've read about sound like?"

"Dude, we've talked about him. He loves mountains and he loves hiking and dune buggies and snowboarding and skiing. Does that sound like the sort of man that likes to go and eat cupcakes?"

"No, I guess not. And actually, he mentioned to me that he'd love to live in the mountains and have a ski cabin, but I absolutely would hate that. I hate snow and I don't know how to ski and I don't know how to snowboard and-"

"Hey, Marcia," Susie cut me off. "Stop talking yourself out of it before it's even happened."

"I'm just saying we don't have anything in common. What's the point?"

"Girl, you're not about to marry the man," Shantal said. "Have some fun. And who knows, maybe if he takes you skiing in the Alps, you just might like it."

"I mean, I wouldn't mind going to the Alps, but only so I could have some Swiss chocolate," I giggled. "But I really need to go. I'm meant to be changing and I told him I would meet him downstairs in 25 minutes. I didn't want to go and hang out with him though about telling you guys. It wasn't that I was keeping it a secret, but I was just a little bit overwhelmed and shocked when I found out that the guy I told to kiss my ass was my boss."

"You what?" They all shrieked.

"What? When did you tell him to kiss your?" Susie's eyes were wide.

"Guys, I'll tell you later, but let's just say I made a huge fool of myself."

"Um, you're going to have to tell us now," Lilian said. "There's no way I'm going to be able to go back to work and not knowing how you told your boss to kiss your ass."

"Well, first of all, I didn't know I was writing it to him. And second of all, I didn't mean to press send."

"You emailed him," Susie said.

"I tried your trick, Susie, and I don't know what happened. Somehow that email got sent."

"Oh my gosh. What did you say?"

"Let's just say none of it was good, but thankfully Finn and I were able to laugh about it."

"Well, that's a good thing he's a good sport," Lilian said.

"Yeah, I have heard that he's a good everything," Shantal said.

"What's that supposed to mean?" Lilian said.

Shantal paused. "I don't know if I should say anything."

"Um, please do."

"So there was this rumor couple of years ago."

"Oh gosh, not another rumor."

"Hey, I'm just saying what I hear. It's up to you if you want to believe it."

"You weren't even working there a couple of years ago," Lillian said.

"How do you know?"

"Let's just say that I started working with this girl called Maria Sanchez and Maria-"

"Really? Lillian said. "Maria Sanchez?"

"Yeah. Why, do you know her?" Shantal said.

"Um, do you know how many Maria Sanchez' there must be in the world? Did you just make that name up?"

"No, I did not make the name up."

"Are you sure?"

"Girl, you want to hear this story or not?"

"Go on," Lilian giggled.

Susie and I just smile at each other. "So anyway, Maria Rosita Sanchez."

"Uh-huh," Lillian said.

"Yeah, well she was good friends with Gloria."

"Oh my gosh. Not Gloria-Gloria," I said.

"Yeah, that Gloria, and Gloria knew all the tea about everything going on because surprise, surprise, she's a gossip."

"That totally doesn't surprise me," I laughed.

"Well, yeah, duh. Anyways, there was this woman that worked for Mr. Winchester. Okay?"

"Okay."

"And she was pregnant."

"Okay."

"And one day."

"Yeah?"

"She snuck her boyfriend into the company and attempted to steal."

"No way. What?"

"Yeah, she attempted to steal five computers, but of course she got caught and Mr. Winchester fired her."

"Okay. And that's bad because why?"

"No, you haven't heard the worst part yet."

"What's the worst part?" I asked.

"Well, the boyfriend took a knife to Mr. Winchester."

"What?"

"Yep, and Mr. Winchester got the knife-"

"Um, I'm going to stop you right there," Lillian, said.

"What?" Shantal said.

"This is starting to sound like an episode of Castle or Law & Order, okay. Someone had a knife and Mr. Winchester took the knife and there was a bunch of laptops or computers being stolen. Like, what does this have to do with anything?"

"I'm just saying that Mr. Winchester then supposedly slept with the lady and the lady then-"

"Oh my gosh, please don't say the lady then tried to pretend that the baby was Mr. Winchester's?"

"What, she did," Shantal said.

"Shantal, you started off the story saying that the lady was already pregnant. How can a pregnant lady convince her boss who she hadn't slept with yet that he was the father of the baby if she was already pregnant before they slept together?"

Shantal paused. "You know, I never thought of about that."

"Oh my gosh. Really, girl?" Lillian started laughing.

"What?" Shantal said. "I guess that just goes to show you, you can't believe everything that you hear."

"Oh my gosh," I groaned. "Shantal, really?"

"What? Just be careful. Okay?"

"Okay," I laughed. "I got to go. Okay? Bye guys."

"Bye."

I hung up the phone and then looked at Susie. "I'm sorry I didn't tell you earlier. I was sort of overwhelmed and I didn't really know what to think or feel, but I really think I like him."

"What changed, Marcia? Like, at the bar, you wanted nothing to do with him. You thought he was just another handsome douchebag. And I know how you feel about dating really good looking, confident guys and ..."

"I know, and of course that sounds stupid and I know that every good looking guy is not going to be an asshole, but I saw a different side to him."

"What do you mean you saw a different side to him?"

"He's really caring. I met this little boy that he is a big brother to and I could tell that that relationship, their friendship, well, it meant something to both of them. And I've never seen anything like that before in my life."

"So you think he's a good guy then?"

"I do. I really do."

"And you think this could go somewhere?" she asked me, staring at me.

"What do you mean?"

"I mean, do you think this could go somewhere? Like, if you had to gamble, would you say yes, it's going to go somewhere more likely than not?"

"I don't know. I barely know the man."

"I know, but," she paused. "Nothing."

"No, Susie, what is it?"

"I'm just saying. If this goes south, like soon, and you lose your job, then we're not going to have any income. And I just don't know that we can go anymore months the way we've been going. I don't have any savings left and I know you don't and ..."

"I understand, Susie. I promise I won't let this jeopardize my job."

"How can you be so sure it won't?"

"I just know, okay. I just know."

TWENTY-FIVE

"I think I'm absolutely stuffed," I said as I ate the last of the cupcakes that we got in that Magnolia bakery. "Those cupcakes were delicious."

"I think they're the best cupcakes I've ever tasted." He ran his hands through his hair and I felt my inner devil wanting to break out.

"You haven't tasted my cupcakes yet."

"True, and you haven't tasted my ding dong." He winked at me and my entire body felt heated. The day was fast turning from PG-13 to Rated R.

"Thank you, Finn. Today has been absolutely wonderful."

"Has it?" He asked me, staring into my eyes as if he were seeking the truth to the universe.

"Yeah, it's been magical," I grinned. "All you have to do is throw some fairy dust in the air now and have Tinker bell flying past my shoulders."

"That can be arranged for a price."

"Money is no object," I said with laugh. "As long as it doesn't cost me more than $5.00."

"I don't know if I can get Tinker bell to show up for less than $5.00. Though maybe if we went to Disney."

"I love Disney. That was one of the best things about living in Florida. Susie and I would go all the time. We had annual passes."

"Oh, yeah? What was your favorite park?"

"Honestly, I loved all of them. There's magic to Disney. I liked going to Magic Kingdom and I loved going to MGM Studios and I loved going to EPCOT. You name it, I loved it."

"I'm not one for theme parks myself," he said as we strolled down the street. "Hey, I was thinking that perhaps I could have you over to my place for a nightcap."

"A nightcap, really, that's what you're calling it?"

"That's what I'm calling what?" He said innocently.

"You're trying to get me back to your place, which you did the other night."

"But this time, this time it's different, though, right?"

"Maybe," I said, smiling. "I mean, are your intentions pure?"

"My intentions have always been pure when it comes to you," he said sweetly.

"Maybe I don't want your intentions to be pure," I said wickedly, smiling up at him. I licked my lips seductively. He'd been a perfect gentleman the entire day and while I loved him for it, I wanted him to be a bit more hands on. I'd wanted him to grab my hand; I'd wanted him to pull me in for a kiss. I'd wanted him to squeeze my ass. I mean, I knew it wasn't appropriate. He wasn't my boss and I wasn't even sure if this was a date or just two people hanging out together, but I knew he was attracted to me and I knew I was attracted to him and I just wanted him to make some sort of move. Did he want me or was this some sort of payback for having rejected him in the first place? I didn't think he was the sort of person to do that, but I didn't know him well enough. Men were like women, they didn't enjoy being scorned, and many of them wanted to make the other pay. I just didn't know if that was what this was for him.

"I was hoping that you'd be a very bad boy with me, Finn Winchester. I was hoping that you wanted me to come back to your place to see, or feel, or touch," I shrugged as I let my words drift off. His eyes narrowed as he started down at my lips and I could feel my heart racing.

"There are many things I'd like to show you. There are many things that I can do to you. I just don't know if you're ready for that."

"Oh, I'm more than ready for that," I said, smiling at him. "I just don't know if you are ready for me."

"I've been ready for you, trust me."

"Can I ask you something, Finn?"

"Sure, ask away."

"What was it about me that you liked when you saw me that first night at the bar?"

"I liked the way that you moved. I liked the way that you carried yourself. I was immediately drawn to your smile and your eyes and the way that you shouted and laughed with Susie. I liked your confidence and your gait. I liked the way that you almost seemed to float through the air. How can one explain such magic?"

I stared at him for a few seconds. "You could've been a poet, you know?"

"No, not really. I'm not a lyricist. I don't have beautiful words. I can't pen sentences together and make people fall in love."

"You sure about that?" I said, as I stepped forward and grabbed his shirt.

"I am," he said huskily as he looked down at me. I stood up on my tippy toes and grabbed his face and pulled him down for a kiss. His lips were arm and lush and I ran my fingers through his hair. He growled as he wrapped his arms around me and I felt his hands on my ass squeezing. I pressed myself against his chest and my breast crushed into the hard, rocks that were his muscles. I shivered slightly as he ran his fingers up my back and then into my hair. He kissed me hard and I slipped my tongue into his mouth. He tasted like blackberries and I moaned softly as he pulled away from me.

"You want us to get a ticket, huh?" He said, almost breathlessly.

"What do you mean?"

"I mean it's illegal to be naked in the streets of New York City."

"But we're not naked."

"If you continue to kiss me like that, we'll be naked very soon." He growled and grabbed my hand. "Come on, let's go."

"Where are we going?" I said.

"Back to my place."

"For a nightcap? I laughed.

"No, we're going back for so much more than a nightcap." He started running and I started jogging next to him.

"I'm going to be out of breath by the time we get back to your place," I said, giggling as we navigated our way through the streets of New York. It was funny because no one even paid any attention to us. It was a normal sight to see a handsome man and a pretty woman running down the streets laughing hand in hand. I wondered if there were anyone watching us wondering what we were up to, where we were going and I realized I didn't care because I was happy and

I'd been wrong. He wasn't cocky or over confident. He was just a handsome man who was blessed with good looks and money and charisma and charm and I was glad he'd spoken to me.

I was glad that I'd been given a second opportunity to get to know him, but what Susie had said resonated in my brain. What if something went wrong? What if everything blew up? Where would that leave me? I could not put Susie in a position of being homeless and I wouldn't want us to have to flee and go back to Florida because of my actions. I stopped gasping for a second and squeezed his hand.

"Tired?" He said.

"A little," I said, "but I'm worried about one thing."

"Yes?"

"I signed that contract and, well, I shouldn't seduce you, I shouldn't kiss you, I shouldn't go back to your place."

"What?" He blinked at me. "You're joking. You literally just told me that," he paused. "What's this about?"

"I'm sorry. I mean, I want you. I really want you," I pressed my hands into his chest. "You're sexy and you're handsome and you're a good guy, but I need this job and I'm already," I signed, "I don't want you to think this is about money."

"I don't," he looked puzzled. "It is about money or it's not?"

"I mean, it is about money, it's about the fact that I need my paycheck to pay my rent and I also signed a contract saying I wouldn't seduce you or be with you, remember? You made me sign it and I can't lose my job if this goes weird or gets weirder and I'm sorry, I should go home."

"What if I gave you $20,000, would that put your mind at ease?"

"No, of course, and I don't want your money. It's not

about the money. I mean, I want to earn the money that I make. I will not take money from you, I'm not one of those women. I'm not a prostitute."

"I didn't say you were a prostitute."

"Then why did you offer me money?"

"Because you're in a bad position and I can afford to-

"No," I cut him off. "Don't give me any money, please."

"What if we rip up the contract? Or," he said, "what if we sign another contract?"

"What do you mean sign another contract?"

"What if we sign a contract that states no matter what happens between us, you have to be given six months notice before you can be fired, does that seem fair?" I chewed on my lower lip.

"I mean, I guess. But what about the seduction part?"

"Oh, that's gone out the window," he laughed. "You do know that any man would want to be seduced by you, Marcia. You're gorgeous. You're funny and you're witty and you're-

"Fine, take me back to your place. You don't have to compliment me anymore."

"What?" He said, "It's not about that."

"I know," I said softly, "and that's why I like you so much. That's why I'm willing to give myself to you," I winked at him.

"You make me hard just saying stuff like that, you know that, right?"

"Oh, really? How hard?"

"Well, come with me and you'll find out."

"Okay, big boy. Take me to your palace."

"Don't get your hopes up, I don't live in Trump Tower."

"What? You mean you don't have a penthouse?"

"I have a penthouse, but let's just say it's modest."

"I bet it's much more extravagant than my place."

"True," he said, "it most probably is. But compared to the Rothschild's or the Vanderbilt's or the Getty's, it's nothing."

"Yeah, well, I don't know them, so that's okay."

"You know what I was thinking?" He said.

"What?"

"One day I'd love to take you to Versailles and show you that palace. You'd be amazed at how beautiful it is."

"I'm sure I would be," I said. "I've always wanted to go to France."

"Maybe one day," he said.

"Maybe." I didn't want to think about things like that. I mean, we barely knew each other. We hadn't even slept together yet. We hadn't even worked together for a full week, and who knew what would happen after we'd had sex, I mean, what if he was the sort of guy that couldn't sleep with a woman and work with her still? I didn't know. That was a chance I was willing to take because I wanted him so badly and he was under my skin and I really wanted my New York moment.

TWENTY-SIX

"Your bed is huge." I walked over to his King sized bed and sat on the edge. I lay back and stared out of the floor to ceiling windows that showcased the entire city.

"That's not the only thing that's huge." He grinned as he ran over and joined me on the bed. He leaned over and pulled me towards him, his lips moving towards mine. His fingers caressed my face and I melted against him, kissing him back with passion.

"Why, Mr. Winchester, I do think you're trying to seduce me." I said in my best Southern accent.

"Why, Ms. Lucas, I do want to be your cock king." His eyes were laughing at me and I pushed him back on the bed.

"I sure hope you're well groomed."

"Would I get in trouble if I said the same?" He growled as he pushed me back onto the bed and rolled on top of me. His lips pressed against my neck and I felt his lips at my ear. "Though, I'd be lying if I said I cared." He whispered huskily. "I want to taste all of you and I don't care if you're bushier than the jungle or not."

"Really, Finn." I laughed giddily as he pulled my dress

up and off of my body. I lay there in my bra and panties and shivered slightly as he looked down at me, his eyes full of lust. His lips pressed against my abdomen and then he licked down towards my belly button. I grabbed his hair and ran my fingers through it, loving the sound of his grunts as he kissed me. He then kissed down to my panties and I moaned as he parted my thighs and continued kissing down my leg to my ankle. I sat up and leaned forward to unbutton his shirt. Once it was off, I stared at his chest in amazement. It was chiseled to perfection; with a smattering of light hair. He had a v going towards his pants and I gestured for him to take them off.

"Already, Ms. Lucas?" He grinned as he jumped up and undid the button on his jeans.

"You don't seem to be complaining."

"I guess I'm not..." He unzipped the jeans and then stepped out of them. He was standing there in a pair of white briefs that complimented his olive skin tone. I swallowed hard at the bulge resting in front of me and I giggled as I watched it twitching and growing. I was eager to see what he was working with, but I didn't want him to think that I was some sort of slut. It was a delicate balance you had to walk when you were a woman. I was all about owning my sexuality and womanhood, but I didn't want to seem too easy. Not that I really cared all that much. Finn and I had played so many games with each other already, that I was ready to finally just have a piece of him. Or all of him. My panties let me know that I wanted every inch of him that he was willing to give.

"Like what you see, Ms. Lucas."

"Yes, Mr. Winchester." I smiled demurely. "Or rather, Mr. Bosshole."

"Really?" He growled as he fell back on to the bed and

pulled me into his arms. I felt his hands on my breasts and I moaned as I reached down to rub his hardness. "Do you still think I'm an asshole?"

"Yes." I giggled as he unhooked my bra. "You're full of yourself."

"Perhaps." His mouth fell to my breasts and he sucked on my nipple as I arched my back. I ran my fingers down his chest and flicked his nipple with my fingernail. He growled as my fingers slipped inside his briefs and I felt the warmth of his cock. I squeezed gently and he froze as I pulled it out. "You'll be the death of me, Marcia."

"I sure hope not." I pushed him back and kissed down his chest. I paused as I gazed at his member. He surely was the cock king. He was thick, long, and clean. I licked my lips and then gently took him into my mouth and sucked. He grunted as I licked his shaft and I felt his body shuddering beneath me as my fingers played with his balls. "Aw fuck, are you trying to make me blow my load immediately?" He reached down and grabbed my hair and moved me away. "I've been dreaming about this since the night that we met." He kissed my lips hard. "Let me make you come first." He slipped his fingers down my panties and I gasped as he rubbed me tenderly and then with more pressure. I closed my eyes as I lay back and felt him kissing down my body. His teeth grabbed the top of my panties and pulled them down my legs. I felt his fingers on my ankles slipping them off of my feet and then I felt his tongue licking up my leg. He growled as he parted my legs and I cried out as I felt his warm breath on me sucking hard. I gripped the sheets as his tongue slid into me. I didn't even have time to process the fact that I was in bed with my boss. Finn Winchester. The yeti himself. The way he worked his tongue made me scream and I heard him chuckling as my body buckled and I came on his face. I couldn't believe I'd orgasmed so quickly. I couldn't believe that his tongue had been better than anything I'd ever had before in my life. If he could do that with his tongue, then I was pretty sure his cock was going to blow my world apart.

"You taste like champagne." He whispered against my parted lips as his fingers played with my nipples. "Are you ready for the king now?"

"If he's not going to blow too soon." I grinned and he kissed me hard before he jumped off of the bed. I watched as he rummaged in the top draw of his nightstand and pulled out a roll of condoms. He ran back to the bed and jumped down next to me, he kissed me all over and ripped open one of the condom wrappers. I watched as he slid it over his hardness and swallowed hard. I wanted this man so badly. It was crazy to think that the first time I'd met him, I'd blown him off and now there was nothing I wanted more than to be with him. It was a lesson I needed to learn. I had to stop judging people based on their looks. It was crazy to think that I'd judged him because he was good looking.

"You're beautiful, Marcia." He grabbed my hands and pulled them up above my head as he positioned himself between my legs. I felt the head of his cock rubbing my clit and I shifted slightly so that I could feel him inside me. He shook his head slightly as he moved his body from side to side, his cock rubbing me and teasing me. I could feel my nipples brushing against his chest lightly as he gripped my hands. I spread my legs wider, needing to feel him inside of me.

"Finn, please," I gasped, as my body grew more and more sensitive to every part of his body that was rubbing against me.

"She walks in beauty, like the night," He said softly. "Of

cloudless climes and starry skies; And all that's best of dark and bright..."

"Finn," I could barely talk as I tried to pull my hands away so that I could grab him.

"Marcia," His eyes were dark with desire. "Meet in her aspect and her eyes; thus mellowed to that tender light..."

"Finn, what?"

"Lord Byron," He grinned, as I felt the tip of him entering inside of me. "Which heaven to gaudy day denies."

"Oh lawd, Finn." I wiggled on the bed as he just stared down at me.

"She walks in beauty."

"Finn." I cried out. "Please."

He leaned down and kissed me hard. I felt his tongue slipping inside my mouth and then with one hard thrust, he was fully inside of me. He increased his pace and I felt my body moving up and down on the bed as he slammed into me. It had never felt like this before. His body felt like fire. I wrapped my legs around his waist so that I could feel him even deeper and it was like we were two dancers, moving to the same beat, in perfect unison. His thumb reached down to rub my clit as he thrust into me and I felt like I'd been transported to another planet. I could barely hold my feelings in. The pleasure coursing through my body was so great that I almost wanted to cry. It felt unbelievable. He felt unbelievable. This was what lovemaking should be. This was a man who knew how to give pleasure. I felt like I was going to pass out. And then he increased his pace. My breasts were slamming against his chest now and he was kissing me harder. He lifted my ass up slightly and repositioned my body and every slam seemed to reach my g-spot. I hadn't even known I had a g-spot. I could hear myself screaming and then he pulled out and flipped me over. I felt

him on top of me, sliding back inside of me. And I lifted my
ass up slightly. He pulled my hair and I screamed as he took
me to the edge. And then I felt myself exploding, gripping
the sheets, and crying out. He increased his pace and I felt
his entire body shuddering on top of me, until he stopped.
We lay there for a few minutes until he pulled out of me
and rolled me back over. He kissed me on the lips and shook
his head.

"That was fucking amazing."

"Yeah, it wasn't so bad." I laughed and yawned as I
reached up and touched the side of his face.

"Not so bad, huh?" His eyes narrowed and he grinned
as he looked down at my naked body. "Maybe you need a
round two."

"Maybe." I giggled and watched as he pulled off the
condom. He stretched and I was about to say something
about the tattoo on his arm when his phone started ringing.
It was the same rap song from before. "Hold on, it's Justin."

"Okay." I nodded.

"Hey Justin, is everything okay?" He answered the
phone and then frowned. "Oh no. I can come and get you.
I'll be right there. No worries." He sighed as he got off of the
phone. "Hey," he smiled at me. "I need to go and get Justin.
He's at a store and having some issues."

"Oh no, is he okay?" I sat up. "Shall I come with you?"

"No, stay here." He smiled. "Make yourself at home."

"I can leave..." I started to get off of the bed.

"No," He licked his lips. "I want you to be here when I
get back."

"Are you sure?"

"More than sure." He grinned. "The Cock King still has
many things to show you."

"Promise?" I lay back and stretched and smiled as he

took a deep intake of breath. He stared at my naked body and growled.

"I want you again already." He shook his head and then leaned down and sucked on a nipple. "Do not leave. That's an order."

"Yes, sir." I laughed as I watched him pulling on his clothes. I couldn't believe that I'd gotten his character so wrong. Finn Winchester was amazing in every single way. And I for one couldn't wait for him to get back so we could spend the rest of the night fucking.

TWENTY-SEVEN

The front door opening roused me from my sleep. I sat up in the bed eagerly; excited to see Finn. I was starting to feel hungry and was hoping he wanted to order some food.

"Darling, I'm here." A sultry voice called out and I frowned. Had a woman entered the apartment? "I'm feeling hot and horny." The voice came closer to the bedroom now and I could feel my face warming. Who the hell was here? "I'm taking off my coat like you asked." A high-pitched giggle sounded and I froze. The bedroom door flew open and a naked lady walked inside wearing nothing but a pair red heels. My jaw dropped as she shimmied back and forth, her red hair swaying back and forth. And then I recognized her. I could feel my body stiffening.

"Abigail?" I said, my voice cracking as the lady stopped moving back and forth. She stared at me in shock. It was her, the lady from the Hilton. What the fuck was going on here?

"You." She pointed at me and made a face. "What are you doing here?"

"What are you doing here?" I said in response as I

stared at her. She didn't even bother trying to cover her body up.

"I'm here to fuck." The words tripped off of her tongue. "Where is he?"

"He's not here." I could barely get the words out. How the hell was she here? They'd acted like they'd never met before. Had they been pretending? Why would he have pretended to never have met her before? Or had that been their first time meeting and he'd already invited her over? Was he just a smooth operator? Was he just a player? Maybe that was his game? He said whatever he thought you wanted to hear so he could get you into bed?

"Why are you here?" She frowned. "Wait, are you going after every guy I'm interested in?"

"No." I shook my head. My head was starting to feel heavy and I knew that I was close to crying. I couldn't believe I'd let my guard down and fallen for another player. When would I learn?

"Well, I'm out of here." She looked disgusted. "Tell him I'll be at the next game."

"Sorry what?" I frowned at her.

"The next baseball game." She rolled her eyes. "Tell him I'll be there and I'll be expecting him to make it up to me."

My jaw dropped at her request. I couldn't believe that she had the gall to ask me to pass on a message to Finn. She didn't wait for me to respond and I watched as she left the room. As soon as she exited, I jumped out of the bed and hurriedly put on my clothes. I wasn't about to wait for Finn to come back now. I'd made a mistake sleeping with him. A huge, huge mistake. I heard the front door slamming and paused, but then realized it was just Abigail leaving. I grabbed my bag and hurried out of the bedroom. I was going to forget that the last 24 hours had even happened. As far as I was concerned Finn Winchester was dead to me as a man. I couldn't afford to walk out of the job, but I could afford to walk out of his apartment and never look back.

"I FRIGGING HATE MEN." I said the millionth time as I sat on the couch watching Too Hot to Handle on Netflix. "These guys are dogs; like really you can't go without sex for 1 day?" I grabbed a handful of popcorn and stuffed it in my mouth. I watched as Susie, Shantal, and Lilian all exchanged looks. "What?" I glared at all of them.

"You don't have to be mad at the world." Susie said softly. "I know you are hurting because of Finn, but—."

"I couldn't care less about Finn Winchester." I shook my head. "He's dead to me."

"Really?" Shantal raised an eyebrow. "He's called you like twenty times in three days right?"

"I'm not counting." I pressed my lips together, but I knew the number was actually fifteen. He had called fifteen times, left three voicemails and sent ten text messages. I hadn't responded to his calls or his texts and had also called in sick to work. I knew I had to go back on Monday and face the music if I wanted to collect my first paycheck, but I wasn't looking forward to it.

"He even stopped by the reception area this morning." Shantal continued. "He asked me if you were okay..."

"What did you say?"

"I said, you were still alive, but very sick." Shantal made a face. "He didn't really seem to buy it, but he didn't push it."

"He's a dog. I can't believe he had that bitch from

Hilton at his apartment, naked." I could feel myself growing heated again. "And let's just say she's not a real redhead."

"Oh? How do you know?" Lilian asked as she sipped on her wine.

"The carpet didn't match the drapes." I rolled my eyes. "Skanky whore."

"Marcia, that's not very nice." Susie said softly.

"I don't care about being nice. She was horrible. The fact that he could even think about sleeping with her and me, well it just shows me that all he cares about is sex. He literally has no standards. Like zero."

"Maybe she's really funny?" Shantal suggested and I just stared at her.

"Trust me, she's not." I grabbed some jellybeans and chewed on them like they were vitamins. My phone started beeping and I looked down at the screen. "It's that asshole again."

"What's he saying?" Lilian asked.

"Marcia, are you okay?" I read out loud. "Please call me." I rolled my eyes. "Yeah, no thanks."

"You should at least allow him the chance to explain." Susie said. "Perhaps there is a reasonable explanation."

"Yeah, he's a manwhore." I grunted. "With his sexy stares and poetry. I did tell you how he recited poetry when we made love, right?"

"A million times." Lilian nodded. "I thought it sounded romantic."

"It's not romantic when he's saying the same five lines to every Bimbo in Manhattan."

"Are you calling yourself a bimbo?" Susie grinned. Her smile faltered as I glared at her. "You should talk to him before you go into work on Monday."

"I have absolutely nothing to say to him."

"Girl, write him an email and let it all out." Susie gave me a look.

"It didn't exactly help the last time."

"I didn't tell you to send that one."

"Fine, I'll write him an email and tell him exactly what I think of him." I got up off of the couch and headed to the front door.

"Uhm, Marcia, where are you going?" Shantal jumped up. "Are we going out?"

"No, I just need some space to think." I sighed. "I'll be back." And before any of them could stop me, I exited the apartment. I could feel tears running down my cheek as I ran down the stairs. I was devastated over what had happened. I felt betrayed and I knew I shouldn't be taking it this hard. It wasn't as if Finn and I had been in an exclusive relationship. It wasn't as if he had committed to me. But it still stung. I'd really liked him and I had started to believe that he had really liked me as well. But I'd been wrong and I'd made a fool of myself. I was done letting my guard down.

TWENTY-EIGHT

Sometimes, I feel like I overanalyze everything in my life too much. Sometimes, I feel like the universe is full of questions that I know none of the answers to. There had been so many times in my life that I wished I'd been able to switch off my heart. So many times in my life when I wished I'd been able to stop the pain. I didn't understand why I felt so hurt. I didn't understand why I felt devastated.

Finn wasn't someone that had promised me anything. He wasn't someone that had said he loved me. He hadn't promised to be my one and only and, yet, I'd really fallen for him. Perhaps, it was because I'd seen the man he was inside. Perhaps, it was because I had seen the tender, caring part of him. But that tender, caring part hadn't been directed towards me. It had been directed towards Justin. Maybe, Finn was the sort of man that could care about others, but wasn't good in relationships. I didn't know what to think. As I walked down the busy Manhattan Street, I realized that I felt homesick. I pulled my phone out of my handbag and decided to call home.

It rang two times and then my father answered, "Marcia, my darling, is that you?"

"Hi, Daddy," I said, softly.

"What's wrong?" he said abruptly and I frowned into the phone.

"What are you talking about, Dad?"

"What's wrong?"

"Nothing's wrong. Why do you say that?"

"I can tell from the tone in your voice that something's wrong. Sweet pea, what is it? Are you homesick? Did someone hurt you? Did something happen?"

My heart melted for my father as I heard the concern in his voice. Before I was able to answer, my mother grabbed the phone.

"Marcia! Marcia, is that you? What's wrong, darling?"

"Nothing's wrong, Mom."

"I heard your dad saying something was wrong. What's wrong? Do you need us to come out there?"

"No, Mom," I said quickly, loving her for how much she loved me and for how overprotective they were. Sometimes, I didn't appreciate it, but, at this moment, I really did. "I just wanted to call you and Dad to see how you were doing."

"We're fine," she said suspiciously. "That's not like you."

"I just wanted to say hello."

"What's wrong?"

"Mom, I already told Dad nothing's wrong. I don't know why-"

"Marcia Lucas, we are your parents. We know you better than you know yourself. Tell me what's wrong."

"Fine," I said, whining into the phone. "It's a guy, okay? I guess I got hurt by a guy and-"

"Oh, my darling," my mother sighed. "He broke your heart?"

"No, I... I don't know," I said softly. "I didn't know him that well, but I thought we had something special, you know?"

"These men, I know," my mother said, sighing. "They will break your heart and then they will break it again. But, when you meet the right man, he will not. Your father, he's never broken my heart."

"I am glad to hear that, Mom."

"So, who is this man? Do I know him?"

"No, Mom. How would you know him? You haven't been to New York yet."

"Well, I want to come and visit you. Me and your father, we can catch a plane tomorrow, if you want?"

"No, Mom. It's okay."

"Hmm," she said. "So, you're not going to see him again, right?"

"Well, um..."

"Marcia, if he breaks your heart, don't see him again. Trust me. You've not learned this from your past relationships? Don't give losers the time of day."

"Mom, I kind of don't have a choice. I have to see him again."

"What do you mean you have to see him again? He lives in your apartment?"

"No, thank God."

"So then?"

"He works with me."

"Oh, I tell you don't get involved with people at work. You don't shit where you eat, Marcia. Ay yai yai. So now, this boy, he's in the same office as you, eh? You competitors?"

"No, we're not competitors."

"Ah, you're his boss."

I started laughing then. My mom was totally in lala land.

"No, Mom, I'm not his boss. You know I'm just a temp at the company."

"Yes. Yes. I looked up the company, Winchester Enterprises. You could go very far. You make a good living there."

"I don't know how far I'll go," I said.

"And why not?"

I debated telling my mom about who had broken my heart. I knew, if I was smart, I most probably wouldn't tell her, but in that moment, all I needed was sympathy.

"Because he's my boss, Mom."

"He's your boss? Oh, no. Ay, Dios mio," she sighed. "Your father needs to talk to you. Marcia, did we not teach you better than this?"

"Yes, Mom. It wasn't like I planned it."

"Ay yai yai. So now you sleep with your boss. What? Do you have to go to HR and you file sexual harassment?"

"No, Mom, it wasn't sexual harassment, and I'm not going to go to HR about him. I don't even think that would matter."

"What do you mean it does not matter? If your boss tries to sleep with you, you go to HR. You tell them. That way the higher ups in the company know."

"Um, there is no one higher up in the company, Mom."

"What do you mean there's no one higher up in the company, eh? He is a manager? He what? Who is he?"

"He's the CEO of the company, Mom. He owns the company."

"Oh, my God. Ay, Dios mio. You slept with Winchester himself?"

"Mom, I never said I slept with him and-"

"Oh, my gosh. You need to talk to your father. You sleep

with an old man. Oh, Marcia! I did not teach you better than... How do you sleep with an old man?"

"Mom, no! No," I started laughing. She was even more dramatic than I remembered. "You've got it wrong, Mom."

"Okay, so you don't sleep with the owner of the company?"

"I never said I slept with him, Mom. I just said he broke my heart."

"Eh. How he break your heart if you not sleep with him, eh? He tell you he think you ugly. Eh, you know that's not true. You're a beautiful girl."

"I know, Mom. And no, he didn't tell me he thought I was ugly."

"So then, how he break your heart, eh? You in third grade? What happened?"

"Okay, so maybe we did kind of kiss and stuff."

"You kind of kiss and stuff, what stuff?

"Okay, so we kind of did stuff, Mom." I groaned. "This is not really what I want to talk to you about."

"Okay, so then, you did sleep with an old man?"

"No, mom! Ugh! Finn Winchester's not old, okay? You must be thinking of his grandfather. His grandfather's no longer the CEO."

"Okay, so the man you sleep with is young."

"Yes, he's young and he's handsome, and I didn't even realize who he was when I first met him, and..." I sighed. "It doesn't matter now. It's just complicated, but he's a dog."

"Oh, so what does he do? He is not good in bed or he say you are not good in bed?"

"Mom! Really?"

"I'm just trying to understand what happened!"

"Mom, he's a player."

"Okay, like how? How is he playing?"

"Mom, I was at his apartment and another woman turned up."

"Oh, so he has multiple girlfriends. Eh, he's rich. That's okay, okay?"

"No, mom, that's not okay! I don't care how rich he is and I wasn't his girlfriend."

"So, you're not his girlfriend, then why are you upset?"

"Mommy, you're not understanding."

"I understand very well, but, Marcia, you know, real life is not books. Real life is not movies, eh? Real life is not reality TV. You watch too much of that. I always said to you, 'Marcia, stop watching so much TV, because you know you going to have false expectations.'"

"Mom, I didn't have false expectations."

"You have false expectations, because you think this man is no good because he has multiple girlfriends, but you are not even his girlfriend."

"Mom, I don't have to be his girlfriend for him not to be sleeping around!"

"Did you have a conversation about this? Eh? You know, men, it takes them long time to fall in love. It take them long time to commit. If you really want to be with him, you give him second chance."

"Mom! Really?"

"What? I'm just saying."

"So, you think I should give him a second chance?"

"Well, he's rich, no?"

"Yeah, I guess he's a billionaire, but what-"

"If he's poor, I say, 'No, kick him to the curb.' But he got money. He got money, you say whatever you want."

"No, Mom. Are you absolutely ridiculous?"

"Eh, I know. I know. You are a very sensitive girl, Marcia, and you are a beautiful girl, so you can be with a man who does not need other women. Maybe not billion-aire, because billionaire have choice of all the beautiful women in the world, but-"

"Thanks, Mom."

"I just tell you the truth, eh? You want to be with a billionaire, then you understand that perhaps it's not a fairy-tale romance, like Romeo and a Juliet."

"Mom, Romeo and Juliet is not the romance that I would personally want. You know that they both die, right?"

"Well, you know, I don't really know the story. I never read it, but you always see people talk about Romeo and Juliet, very, very happy."

"Mom, no one talks about Romeo and Juliet being very, very happy." I realized I was starting to get frustrated. "Any-way, Mom, I just called because I wanted to say hello. Thanks very much for your... concern about my broken heart."

"Oh, Marcia, you know we love you very much, and, if you want to come home, we pay for your tickets. If you want for us to come, we come and we take care of you, eh?"

"I know, Mom."

"We love you, Marcia, very, very much. You are a beau-tiful daughter."

"I love you too, Mom. Okay? I'll speak to you later."

"Bye, Marcia. You want to say goodbye to your father?"

"Not now, mom." I hung up quickly before she could put my dad back on the phone. That hadn't gone exactly as I'd planned. I loved my parents very, very much, but, every time I spoke to them, I realized that we were just on two very completely different planets.

My phone started ringing again and I rolled my eyes. I looked at the screen, expecting it to be my parents calling back. I froze as I realized that it was Finn. *Don't pick up.*

Don't pick up. But, maybe it was the conversation I just had with my mom that energized me, but I answered it.

"What do you want?" I said, as I picked up the phone.

"Marcia," he sounded surprised. "Are you okay?"

"I'm fine. Finn, is that you?"

"Yeah, it's me. I was just calling to make sure that you weren't too sick. I saw that you called out and-"

"Yeah, I'm feeling better. I'll be at work on Monday."

"Um, I'm a little bit confused here, Marcia. Can we-"

"What are you confused about, Finn?"

"Um, I'm confused, because you were at my apartment just a couple of days ago and we made love and I said I'd be right back and, when I got back, you were gone and I haven't been able to get in contact with you since."

"Well, that's life, right?"

"Are you like the female version of Dr. Jekyll and Mr. Hyde?" he said, confused. "I mean, I don't really understand what's going on here."

"You don't understand what's going on? Maybe, just maybe, I don't understand what's going on."

"You're not making any sense."

"I'm not making any sense? You're not making any sense."

"Marcia." He cleared his throat. "Is it possible for me to come over and see you? Can we talk? Can we-"

"You don't want to see Abigail?"

"Sorry, what?"

"I said, you don't want to see your redheaded vixen who, by the way, is not a natural redhead. I'm guessing Clairol."

"Um, I don't know what you're talking about. Are you on drugs right now, Marcia?"

"No, I'm not on fucking drugs, Finn." I could feel myself growing angry. "Anyway, I have to go."

"Wait, Marcia!" he said. "I'm really, really confused, and I was hanging out with Justin today and he was wondering where you were because he'd invited you to come and join us this weekend. I don't know if you forgot, but-"

"I didn't forget, but I don't feel like I want to go."

"Okay, because... the sex was that bad or...?"

"What?" I said.

"Is this because the sex was bad? I mean, I thought the sex was good, but-"

"You know what? Is this all about sex to you? That's all you care about, right? You just can't keep it in your fucking pants. You go from me to Abigail, to whomever... Who knows who else?"

"I don't know what you're talking about. Abigail who?"

"From the Hilton."

"Oh." He sounded surprised. "That redhead that was flirting with me?"

"Yeah, the one that you gave your number to and the one that you gave a key to your apartment to."

"What are you talking about? A key to my apartment?"

"How do you get into your apartment?"

"Well, there's a number pad, so there are no keys."

"Okay, so you gave her the code. That's even worse."

"We need to talk in person, Marcia. Can we-"

"I got to go. Bye."

I hung up and stood at the corner of the street, staring at the phone. Well, that conversation hadn't gone as planned either. I couldn't believe that he was acting like he didn't know Abigail had gone to his apartment. She'd been freaking naked. Like, why else did he think she'd gone? Unless he was going to try and say it was some sort of business meeting and he didn't realize she was going to be naked. I chewed on my lower lip for a couple of seconds.

Maybe, just maybe, he hadn't known. Maybe, she'd gone to seduce him and he was just the stupid guy that given a psycho his key code. But no, that didn't make sense. Why would he meet her at his apartment unless it was for sex? Why not meet her at the office? And then why pretend he didn't even remember who she was? No, he was just a dog and a liar like every other guy.

My phone started ringing again and I saw it was him. I sighed and then sent him to voicemail before powering the phone off. I was done with this bullshit. I wasn't going to listen to him try and gaslight me. I didn't need that in my life. My mom thought I should accept it because he was rich, but I didn't need a rich man. I just wanted a man that would love me and treat me well. I just wanted a man that only wanted to be with me. And that certainly wasn't Finn Winchester. I wasn't going to play his games. I wasn't going to let him make me think I was crazy. I wasn't going to settle for less. I'd left Florida because a guy had made me feel like shit about myself, and I sure as hell wasn't going to date a guy in New York that made me feel the exact same way, even if he was Finn Winchester.

TWENTY-NINE

The sound of the TV in the background woke me up early the next morning. I yawned and stretched as I opened my eyes. "What are you watching Susie?" I shouted in annoyance.

"Sorry," she called back. "Did the TV wake you up?"

"Yeah, it did." I knew I had an attitude, but I couldn't stop myself.

"My bad, but it is almost noon," she said as she walked over to me. "Are you okay, Marcia?"

"I'm fine."

"Well, you're certainly not acting fine. I know you're really upset over what has gone down with Finn. I know that he really hurt you and I know that you are in pain, but you need to really stop taking it out on everyone else because it's not our fault. And maybe you should speak to him and-"

"I spoke to him last night. Okay. He pretended like he didn't even know that Abigail had gone over."

"Oh", she said, "I'm sorry. I feel guilty, I feel like this is my fault."

"Why would it be your fault, Susie? It's not your fault at all. I'm the one that slept with him."

"I'm the one that told you to give him a chance. I'm the one that said you shouldn't judge a book by its cover, that not all good-looking guys were bad news. And obviously I was wrong because Finn is super bad news. I feel like if I hadn't told you to let your guard down, then you wouldn't have given him a chance and-"

"Oh Susie, please." I sat up and grabbed her hand. "This is really not your fault, okay. Trust me. He was charismatic and handsome and funny. I thought he was a good guy. And you know what? Maybe in some areas of his life, he is. But he just wasn't a good guy for me to mess around with," I shrugged. "I really didn't like the fact that he was trying to gaslight me."

"How was he gaslighting you?" she asked me, raising an eyebrow.

"Pretending he didn't even know who Abigail was and that everything was in my head, like why I was upset. And..."

"Oh, so you said that Abigail had come over to sleep with him and he pretended he didn't know?"

"Yep. He had no clue. Well, I didn't exactly say those words, but-"

"What do you mean you didn't exactly say those words? What did you say?"

"I can't remember what I said exactly, but I did bring up Abigail."

"You told him that she showed up at the apartment and?"

"I can't remember exactly what I said. Does it matter?"

"I guess not," she said. She looked down at the newspaper in her hands and folded it quickly as she saw I was glancing at her.

"What is it?"

"Nothing," she shook her head.

"Oh my gosh. Is he in the newspaper with Abigail right now?"

"No, not at all."

"Then why do you look so guilty?"

"He is in the newspaper, but not with Abigail."

"Who's he in the newspaper with then?"

"I don't know, some baseball player," she showed me the front cover. It was a photo of Finn and a handsome guy. "Who's that?"

"I don't know," she said. "You know I don't care about baseball."

"Yeah, me either. Why didn't you want me to see it?"

"Because I didn't want you to think that he was going on with his life and having a good time".

"Girl, I'm sure he is. He doesn't care that I'm not speaking to him. He most probably fucked some other girl last night. He's gorgeous and he is rich. What does he need with me?"

"Yeah, I guess. I'm sorry, girl."

"That's fine," I sighed. "I guess I just have to live with it. But you know what?"

"No. What?" she said.

"Originally I was done with really good looking guys."

"Yeah."

"Well now I'm also done with really rich guys as well."

"Oh my gosh. Really, Marcia don't you think that's being a bit extreme."

"Nope. You can't trust really good-looking guys. And you can't trust really rich guys."

"I don't know if that's true. I-"

"'Trust me, girl. It's true."

"I really don't want..."

"I know you don't want to believe it, but trust me I know."

"Okay, girl. If you..." The doorbell rang and we both stared at each other.

"Are you expecting anyone?" I asked her.

"No, you?"

"No one. Maybe Shantal or Lilian decided to come over?"

"I don't think so," she shook her head. "But I guess I'll go and see." She walked to the front door and opened it. "Hello?" "Oh", she said, and I heard a deep voice.

"Who is it?" I called out.

"It's me." The familiar voice sounded through the room and I sat up in shock. Was that Finn? What was Finn doing at my apartment? I jumped out of bed and ran towards the front door. "What are you doing here?" I said glaring at him.

"I came to talk to you."

He looked like he had just woken up. His hair was still wet from the shower. And he was wearing a gray T-shirt and blue jeans. He looked even more handsome than I remembered. And I hated myself for still being attracted to him. "I didn't invite you over Finn, so?"

"I don't care that you didn't invite me over. We need to talk."

"No, we don't actually, I-"

"Yeah, we do. You don't have a phone call with me like you did last night and hang up on me and think we're not going to have a conversation."

"Well, I don't want to have a conversation with you. I will see you at work tomorrow and-"

"Marcia Lucas. We need to talk." He turned around and looked at Susie, "I don't suppose that Marcia and I could chat privately for a little bit. Maybe you could go and get breakfast?"

"What?" she stared at him, and then she stared at me. I shook my head and she sighed, "Fine. I'll be gone for an hour."

"Thank you," he said, and pulled out a couple of $20 notes and handed them to her. "Breakfast on me."

"No, I'm not going to-"

"Please. I'm kicking you out of your own home. And I hate to do that, but I really need to speak to Marcia and sort everything out before work on Monday."

"Fine", she said. "Do you want anything Marcia?"

"No, I wouldn't eat anything paid for by his blood money."

"My blood money?" he raised an eyebrow. "You're certainly very dramatic today."

"I'm dramatic? Really you're the loser that tried to gaslight me?"

"And with that, I'm out of here". Susie made a face and left the apartment. The door closed behind her.

I walked over to Finn and poked him in the chest. "What the hell do you think you're doing here? Did I say that you could come to my private space? In fact, how did you even get my address? I never gave it to you."

"Are you joking Marcia?"

"What do you mean am I joking? No. Are you stalking me or-"

"You work for me. Your address is in my database."

"Oh yeah," I said, feeling like a little bit of a fool. "Well, that didn't mean you could access the database and just come here and-"

"We need to chat."

"Why? I already said everything I have to say to you. You're a dog and-"

"I really wish that you trusted me enough to-"

"Excuse me," I cut him off. "I don't need to trust you. I know that..."

He took a deep breath, "Marcia. I think I know what this is about." He shook his head and sighed, "It's my own fault, I should have told you."

"Told me what?"

"I should have told you that Brody was staying at my apartment for a couple of weeks."

"Who the hell is Brody and what does he have to do with anything?"

"Brody is a friend of mine. He's a baseball player. He just got traded to play for the New York Yankees. And he hasn't got a place yet. He's been staying at my apartment."

"Okay. And?"

"And it turns out that he met a certain redhead a couple of nights ago and invited her over."

"Okay. And?"

"And he gave her the entry code and he forgot that he'd invited her and he didn't tell me."

"What are you talking about?" Then suddenly it dawned on me. "Abigail? He invited Abigail over?"

"Yes," he nodded, "I didn't invite her over. I'd never met her until that day at the Hilton."

"I thought that was weird that you pretended that you didn't know each other when you met, but then-"

"We'd never met before and I've never seen or spoken to her after that day. It's just a horrible coincidence that she's the same woman that Brody met at a club the other night and invited back."

"She came to see your friend and not you?" I stared at him with disbelief. "Really?"

"Really. What sort of guy do you think I am? She didn't come for me. I don't know how to prove it to you, I just think that you should believe me, but if you want, we can speak to Brody and he can also tell you."

Then I remembered what Abigail had said to me when we're in the department, she'd said, "Tell him, I'll see him at the game". Fuck it made sense. "She went to see your friend, the baseball player. Didn't she?"

"That's what I just said," he nodded.

"Was there a baseball game recently?"

"Yeah, there was one yesterday," he said.

"Did she go to that game?"

"I don't know. I don't have any contact with her."

"But did you see her with Brody or?"

"There are many women that are after Brody and he sometimes gives his number out when he shouldn't," he sighed. "He gets himself into trouble and now it looks like he's getting me into trouble."

"Oh shit, so she really didn't go for you?" I felt absolutely awful. I completely overreacted. He hadn't done anything wrong.

"I can see that you believe me now," he said, sighing as he sat down on the couch. "I don't know why you wouldn't have spoken to me about this instead of just freezing me out Marcia."

"I know. I'm sorry. I just..." I let out a deep sigh. "I've been hurt so many times in the past and I just automatically assumed the worst. What would you think if you were in my bed and some man busted in naked saying he was here to screw?"

"I'd think that there was a perfectly reasonable explanation," he said.

"Really?"

"Okay. I can understand why you might think she was there for me. I hadn't told you that Brody was staying with me. So you didn't know that she could have been there for someone else, but I really wish you would've spoken to me. Communication is the key if we're going to have a real relationship."

"A real relationship?" I stared at him in surprise. "What do you mean?"

"What do you think I mean, Marcia?"

"I don't really know." My heart was fluttering now. What was he saying?

"I thought that we were both on the same page when we slept with each other. I thought we both liked each other and we wanted to see where this was going."

"You like me?" I couldn't believe what I was hearing.

"Yeah. Even though you're crazy and even though you don't communicate well, and even though you jump to assumptions really, really quickly, I like you Marcia. I think you're fun and funny and spunky and beautiful. There's something about you that I'm just drawn to," he sighed. "I don't know if perhaps I'm crazy."

"Why would you say that?" I said glaring at him.

"Because you're not giving me many reasons to fall for you."

"I know, I'm sorry," I cut him off. "I really like you. I think I'm falling for you and that's why it hurt me so much. And-"

"You're falling for me?" he said. A glint in his eyes.

"Yeah, I guess so. I think I've been falling for you for a while now. I really think you're a great guy and I was just taken aback when I thought that you had another woman coming over. But now I realize that that wasn't true. I feel like a fool and I'm sorry. I understand if you think that I'm immature, and I understand if you think that you can't trust me. But I promise if we give this another go, that if there's any... if there's ever a time that I have questions, I will come to you and I will ask you what's going on before I jump to conclusions."

"You promise me that?" he said with a grin.

"I promise."

"You know, I think you are the world Marcia. But I have one condition for you before we jump back into this."

"Yes. I'll sleep with you again," I grinned at him.

"No, that's not the condition."

"What is?"

"Let's go camping."

"What?" I made a face. "What do you mean?"

"Tomorrow, let's fly to San Francisco and we'll drive up to Yosemite and we'll go camping. I scored permit tickets to climb half dome. I think it would be a really fun experience to have with you."

"Half what?" I said.

"It's a hike."

"Oh my God. I don't like hiking, I..."

"I promise if you can't finish it, we'll stop and we'll turn back."

"But we got to go camping, can't we just do the quick hike and then go to a hotel."

"The experience is camping, Marcia."

"Fine," I said. But only on one condition."

"So you're giving me a condition for my condition?" he laughed.

"Yeah, I am."

"What's your condition?"

"Make love to me," I said, leaning forward and pressing my lips against his. I was no longer able to keep my hands off of him. "Make love to me and then I'll go camping with you."

"You don't have to ask me twice," he said, as he pulled me into his arms.

THIRTY

"I just want to lick and taste you all over," he whispered in my ear as he pulled off my top.

"Finn, really? I don't know that this is the right time or place."

"You just asked me to make love to you, Marcia I take my responsibilities very seriously."

"But yeah, Susie could walk in at any moment."

"She said she'd be gone for an hour." He pressed his lips against my hair. "Doesn't it make it just that little bit more exciting to know she could walk in at any moment?"

"No," I said, pushing him away. "It doesn't make it exciting knowing that my best friend and roommate could walk in on me having sex."

"Then I guess we should be fast." He said, his lips now moving to mine. He pulled me into his arms and kissed me passionately, and I kissed him back, not able to stop myself. My fingers ran down the side of his body and squeezed his muscular arms. He pulled his t-shirt off and I pressed my lips against his chest and kissed all the way down to his stomach. He grinned as he looked at me and I grinned back.

"I missed kissing you," I said, and he laughed.

"I missed you kissing me and I missed kissing you as well. Don't ever let us not talk for that long again. Okay?"

Did you really miss me that much?" I said in surprise.

"More than you'll ever know." He nodded. "I was so worried. I just didn't understand what happened. I thought that it was me that you had changed your mind about. I thought that you regretted having sex with me. I thought that the sex had been bad. I..."

"You didn't really think the sex was bad, did you?"

"No," he laughed. "I didn't."

"Really, Finn?"

"What?

"You were crying and screaming."

"And remember I felt how wet you were and I felt how many orgasms you had and ... "

"Okay," I said, blushing. "Fine. What?"

"So I kind of knew the sex was good, but maybe I thought to myself, "Was the sex too good. Did I scare you?"

"How can you scare me because the sex is too good?"

"I don't know. You're a complicated woman, Marcia."

"That I am. You'll have to remember that."

"I remember everything about you," he said softly. "Now, take off your clothes quickly."

"Well, you do the same." I said.

"Okay," and I watched as he jumped top and pulled all his clothes off within seconds. "Something tells me you've practiced that."

"Maybe," he said. He got down in my bed and I pressed my body against his. We touched each other slowly, lightly at first, just playing with each other's body, studying each other, just enjoying being with each other.

"I feel like a fool," I admitted softly, as his fingers played with my nipples and I purred against him. "I shouldn't have assumed the worst. I ... "

"It's okay, Marcia. We'll put this past us. We both made mistakes and we'll try not to make them in the future."

So this guy Brody, is he still staying with you? Is he..."?

"I told him he needs to get his own place." He chuckled. "Or stay in a hotel room."

"Okay. That's good."

"Yeah. I didn't want anything like this to happen again. I would never want you to think that I would ever sleep with you and try and be with another woman at the same time."

I mean you don't have to explain yourself to me. You-"

"Yes, I do, Marcia. I hope you know that I want you to be my girlfriend. I hope you know that this isn't something I'm taking lightly."

My heart raced for a few seconds as I stared at him. "Are you sure? I don't want you to feel like you're rushing into something."

"From the moment I saw you, from the moment I realized that you were working at my company, I knew I had a decision to make and I made it already. This is something I'm pursuing seriously. You are someone I'm pursuing seriously." He kissed me on the lips. "I really like you, Marcia. In fact, I..." He paused. "I don't know if I should say this. I don't want to scare you off."

"Say what?" I said, almost breathlessly, my heart stopping.

"I think I'm falling in love with you, Marcia Lucas."

"Really?" I squeaked, staring back at him.

"Really." He nodded.

"I think I'm falling in love with you as well, Finn Winchester." I kissed him passionately and he growled as he pulled me down on top of him. We rolled around on the bed. I could feel his cock growing beneath me and I moaned as I rubbed back and forth on him, grinding.

"Fuck, I'm so hard." He said.

"I know," I giggled. "It's my turn now," I said, as I went to him.

"Your turn?"

"Yeah, I want to be on top." I positioned myself over him and rubbed back and forth so that the tip of his cock was hitting my clit. He groaned as I leaned forward and brushed my nipples against his lips and he reached up and sucked. I moaned as I felt his finger between my legs, rubbing my clit and so I was wet. "Do you have a condom on you?" I said, softly, and he nodded, reaching down to the ground and pulling one out of his jean pocket. I didn't ask him why he had condoms in his pocket. He was a man and maybe I just didn't want to know the answer. He ripped the packet open and slipped the condom down on his now hard cock, and I positioned it back between my legs and gently lifted myself up and lowered myself on him.

He grunted as I started gyrating my hips, moving back and forth on him.

"Don't stop," he said, as he grabbed my hips and moved me up and down faster and faster. I cried out as I slammed down into him and felt the full length of his cock inside of me. He reached up and played with my nipples as I bounced up and down on him, and we both froze as we heard a noise outside the door. I would absolutely die if Susie walked in and saw me like this, but thankfully the door didn't open.

"We need to hurry," I said, crying out as I moved back and forth in him. He nodded and reached up and kissed me. Before I knew what was happening, he had pulled me off of him and positioned me back down on the bed so that my ass was up in the air. He moved behind me and thrust inside of me so that we were now doing doggy style. I felt him even deeper inside of me and cried out as every time he slammed inside of me, I could feel him rubbing against my G-spot. I leaned forward and gripped the sheets as I felt myself coming. I screamed his name for him to go faster and faster and then I felt him coming as well. He grabbed my hips as he slammed one final time inside of me and I felt his body shuttering behind me. He pulled out and pulled me into his arms and kissed me passionately.

"That was fucking hot," He said.

"Yes." I gasped, barely able to talk. "That was amazing."

"Not as amazing as it would be when we go camping tomorrow," he said.

"Oh, don't remind me." I laughed as we lay there, just staring at each other. Then the door opened and we both froze. Susie walked in with a bag of donuts and stood there.

"Oh my gosh," she said, a half smile on her face. "I'm guessing you guys made up?"

"Yeah. Oh my God. I'm so sorry, Susie."

"It's okay." She shook her head. "I guess I can leave again. Should I come back in another hour or-"

"No. It's okay." Finn shook his head. "In fact, if you're interested, we're going to San Francisco tomorrow. We're going to go camping.

"Um, okay." She shrugged. "What does that have to do with me?"

"Maybe you'd like to join us?" I stared at him in surprise. "Oh, yeah. I forgot to tell you." He grinned at me. "Brody's coming."

"Who's Brody," Susie asked, curiously.

"My friend." He said. "He's a baseball player."

"He's a player," I said to Susie. "He's the one that Abigail had come to bang."

"Oh." Susie's eyes widened. "Okay then."

"So would you like to come with?" He said. "It'll be fun. We're going to climb Half Dome and we'll enjoy some good food in San Francisco."

"Come on, Susie. Please. I don't want to be with Finn and his friend without you." I glared at Finn. "And thanks for not telling me that your friend was coming. When was I going to find this out?"

"On the plane," He grinned, winking at me.

I rolled my eyes. "Please, Susie."

"I guess," she said. "I guess I don't really have anything else going on."

"Yay! Awesome." I kissed Finn on the lips and then hit him in the shoulder. "You need to put your clothes on now. Susie, do you mind giving us a couple of minutes whilst we get dressed?"

"Don't worry." She said, and then sighed. "You know what? I think I will go out and I'll be back later."

"Where are you going?" I asked her.

"Well, if I'm going camping, I need to get some hiking boots." She grinned.

"But money?"

"I've got some savings," she laughed.

"What do you mean?"

"An emergency fund." She grinned. "For times like this."

"Oh, Susie." I laughed. "Really?"

"What? I couldn't let you know about every single penny I had," and with that she left the apartment. I stared at Finn and laughed as he jumped up and pulled on his clothes. "Where do you think you're going, young man?"

"You just told me to get dressed."

That was before I knew Susie was leaving. Now that she's gone, well, we have time for round two."

He looked at me, shook his head and crawled back into bed. "You're a nympho, aren't you, Marcia Lucas."

"Maybe," I said. "Or maybe I'm just a nympho with you. You are the cock king after all."

"Well, thank you. I don't think I've ever been called a name I appreciate more." He said, and then we both started laughing.

THIRTY-ONE

"So then I was telling him that I'm not going to sign for $5 million. I'm not going to sign for $6 million. I'm only going to do it for $10 million." Brody was muttering something to Finn, and I sat there trying not to look shocked. Brody, Finn and I were sitting in the first class lounge waiting for Susie to arrive. She hadn't come with us to the airport because she had gotten an interview at the last moment and wanted to go to that first.

I sat there staring at Brody. He was a handsome man, a very, very handsome man with hazel green eyes and dark hair and a baseball player's body. But it was very obvious to me that he knew how handsome he was. I'd seen plenty of women eyeing him as they walked by and he had been eyeing them as well. I thanked the Lord that Finn wasn't the sort of guy to check out other women. I squeezed his hand as we sat there and he smiled at me, a curious expression on his face. And I just smiled back. I didn't want to let him know just how much I appreciated who he was as a person. He was a really good, solid guy and I loved being around him and spending time with him. Almost as much as I loved making love with him.

"Oh my gosh. There you are. Marcia", Susie said.

I looked up and saw my best friend as she hurried towards us, a black suitcase in her hands.

"There you are." I jumped up and gave her a hug. "I was beginning to wonder if you were going to make it."

"I'm here", she said. "You know, I said, I would try and I'm here". She beamed at me and then she looked at Finn, "Hi." She looked at Brody and was about to say something when he started talking, "Oh shit, come on now, Finn", Brody said. "I mean I know I'm single. And I know there are a lot of women that want to be with me, but you could have told me you were trying to hook me up. I mean, I thought I was just going on a hike. I didn't realize that I was going to have to entertain a woman." He looked at Susie, "It's nice to meet you, dear, but I'm not really looking for anything this weekend."

"What?" She said, blinking and looking at me. "What is this guy talking about?"

"I have no idea." I looked at Finn, he was shaking his head. "Dude. This is Susie she's Marcia's best friend."

"Okay. And like I said, she's not here as a hookup for you, dude. She's just coming to enjoy the trip with us as Marcia's best friend."

"Oh, okay." He looked her up and down.

She glared at him. "I had a bad feeling. This was going to be a really long week in San Francisco."

"Let's go and get a drink", I said, looking at Susie and then back at Finn. "Excuse us."

"Okay", Finn said with a nod. I hurried away and Susie looked at me with an annoyed expression.

"Please tell me that guy is not going to be with us, the entire trip."

"Yeah. He's one of Finn's best friends."

"He's a jerk, Marcia. I do not want to spend a second with him", Susie said softly.

"I know he doesn't seem like the most fun, but if he's best friends with Finn he's-"

"What does that mean? Guys have horrible tastes when it comes to friends", she groaned. "Wait who did he think he was making those comments to me. He thought I was coming on this trip to be with him? He thinks he's some sort of god? Some baseball player? Whatever, jackass. I'm not interested in you; I would never be interested in you. No, not even if he was the last man on earth, would I want to be with him."

"I know girl. You can do so much better than him."

"Yeah. You can say that again. He better not try and say anything to me or do anything or come on to me, or", she said. "I don't know if this is a good idea. I think I should go home."

"Please, Susie. No, no, please. I can't be stuck this weekend with him."

"See, you don't even like him either."

"I mean, he seems like he's charismatic and he seems like he's fun, but",

"But what?"

"Yeah, I don't just want it to be me, him and Finn. I admit it. I need you please."

"You owe me Marcia."

"I know. I promise, I will make it up to you."

"Well, just don't leave me alone with him, okay?"

"I won't."

" Promise?"

"Yes. I already told you I promise."

"Fine", she said, "I mean, he is kind of cute though. Don't you think?"

"Marcia", Susie glared at me.

"What? I'm just making a comment. He could be fun for a weekend fling or something."

"Girl. No", Susie said. "Never in a million years."

"That's what I said, and look at me and Finn."

"Trust me. That guy is no Finn Winchester."

Susie rolled her eyes and I couldn't help but agree.

"Okay. This is the campsite", Finn said, as we pulled up to a campsite. He started unpacking some tents and sleeping bags and Susie and I just stood there looking at him. "Wow. This is really not what I expected", I said, as I looked around. It was beautiful. I could see trees everywhere and I felt I could hear a stream in the distance, but I also felt it was really remote and scary.

"We didn't see a restaurant for a long time", I said. "What are we supposed to eat?"

"That's why we stopped at the grocery store, dear", Finn laughed. "We're going to cook."

"Where?"

"On the campfire."

"Okay. Are there bears here?" I said looking around. Susie was looking around as well.

"Yeah, but they most probably won't come to the campsite." Finn grinned.

"It's okay. I'll protect you."

"Okay." I wrapped my arms around him and kissed him on the cheek. "You better."

"I will. My dear." He kissed me on the forehead.

"Okay. So we'll put our tent here", he pointed to one

spot. "And then Susie, your and Brody's tent will go over there.

"Wait, what?" Susie piped up. "What do you mean mine and Brody's tent?"

"What do you mean?" Finn was confused. "You guys are sharing a tent."

"I'm not a tent with him." She glared at Brody, who was silently laughing. "It's not funny, dude."

"I'm not laughing at you. I'm just laughing at the situation. Would you rather just sleep in your sleeping bag in no tent?"

"No. I thought I was going to share a tent with Marcia and you two would share a tent."

"No", Finn shook his head and then looked at me, "I mean I wanted this to be a romantic weekend for us. And how are we going to have fun in our sleeping bags if you are in a different tent", he said. I chewed on my lower lip. The only positive part about this trip for me was being with Finn. But I felt guilty because I knew how much Susie didn't want to be in a tent with Brody.

"Susie, it'll be fine if you share a tent with Brody."

"What? I thought we", her voice trailed off and she shook her head. "You really owe me Marcia Lucas."

"I know", I said. "It'll be fine."

"Yeah. Trust me", Brody piped up. "You don't have to worry about me. It's not like I'm going to try and seduce you."

"Okay", Susie rolled her eyes. "It's not like I'm going to try and seduce you either."

"Sure", he said. "Sure you're not."

"Really. Is this a joke? Am I being punked here?" I stared at Finn.

"Brody, knock it off, okay?"

"What?" Brody shrugged. "I'm just saying, all the women want me."

"All the? I don't want you Brody. Get that through your thick head", Susie said, and I got to her. I'd never seen her speaking to anyone like that before, but I understood why she chose to speak that way to Brody. He was really being an asshole.

"Dude. What is up with your friend?" I said to Finn.

"Don't mind him", Finn whispered in my ear. "He had some bad news recently and I think he's overcompensating."

"What bad news?"

"It's to do with the Yankees, but we'll talk later."

"Okay. Fine."

"I'm so glad you're here", he smiled at me as he looked around. "I have wanted to be in nature with you for so long. Do you absolutely hate it?" He said softly.

"No." I smiled at him and looked around. "I know you love being in the mountains, and honestly I love hearing the sound of the birds in their natural habitat. I love hearing the stream in the distance. I love being among the trees and in nature. It's so very different to the city. It's beautiful." I said softly. "And if you love it, I will learn to love as well, because it doesn't matter where I am as long as I'm with you."

"Or really", he said.

"Really", I nodded. "You matter to me more than the place. Being with you feels like home. I know that feels weird to say, but it's true."

"You're absolutely amazing, you know that Marcia? You are just perfect for me."

"I don't know about that. I",

"You are", he says. He kissed me on the lips. "You are one in a million."

"No, I think you are one in a million."

"Maybe we're both one in a million", he said softly. "And maybe one day we can move to the mountains. But",

"But what", I said.

"Not until you figure out your documentary career and what you want to do with that." His eyes shone, "because I want you to be happy. I want you to explore your dreams and your goals, and I'll be there supporting you every step of the way."

"You're serious", I said.

"I've never been more serious in my life. I love you Marcia. I know I said that. I thought I was falling in love with you but I've already fallen. I've already fallen, hook, line and sinker and there's nothing more than I want in the world than to be with you."

"I love you, Finn Winchester. I love you more than words couldn't say." I grabbed him and I kissed him hard and he wrapped his arms around me and swung me around. It was only then that I noticed that both Susie and Brody were clapping and cheering for us.

"Oops, sorry about that", I said grinning.

"No worries", Susie said. "I'm happy for you. I'm really and truly happy for you."

"Thank you." I smiled at her softly and squeezed Finn's hand. I was the happiest I'd ever been in my life and as I stood there, staring at Susie and staring at Brody, who was staring at Susie. I wondered if perhaps, just maybe, Susie could find the same love that I had as well.

BONUS CHAPTER

A scene from Finn's POV

I hadn't been in a bar by myself in months. It felt nice to blend in with the ground. Noone here knew or cared who I was. I was going to get a beer or two, listen to the hard rock that was playing through the jukebox and just watch the citizens of New York City do their thing. Sometimes I hated the noise and the bustle of people. I much preferred the solitude of nature. The still beauty of the mountains. But still, sometimes it was nice to be among people. I stood by the bar and surveyed the crowd idly and then the room almost seemed to still, the crowds blurred and only one person stood out. She moved gracefully, a confidence to her gait as she passed a group of college guys who were catcalling to her and her friend. She had shoulder length straight black hair, dark brown eyes, a beautiful smile and slender body. She was wearing a black dress that fit her like a glove. I could feel my heart racing as she headed towards me. She was a vision unlike any I'd seen before. I watched as she quickened her pace and spoke to her friend, "there's an open space at the front." I realized she was talking about the spot next to me and I grinned.

She stopped next to me; yet she didn't make eye contact. Her friend excused herself to go to the bathroom and I knew that this was my moment to talk to her. Though I wasn't sure what to say, so I just stared at her. She was beautiful. And for some reason I couldn't put my finger on, she made my heart race.

"Hi?" She suddenly turned to look up at me and gave me a questioning smile. Her lips were painted a blood red and I couldn't stop from staring at them. "See something you like?" She continued, giving me a teasing smile. I wanted to laugh out-loud. She was funny.

"I don't really know how to take that comment." I looked her up and down. I knew I was being forward, but she was gorgeous. I wanted her name and her number. I wanted to take her on a date. I wanted to get to know this gorgeous woman. Was this what love at first sight felt like? And was she feeling the same way? "Why? Do you see something you like?" I teased her back.

"Yes," She said with a confident gaze and I grinned at her. Then she pointed at the bottles behind the bar. "Lots and lots of alcohol."

"Touché," I couldn't stop myself from laughing. This brunette beauty had caught my attention. Maybe I wouldn't have to spend the night alone, after all. "Nice to meet you." I was about to ask if I could buy her a drink. I almost started laughing at how nervous I felt. This was so unlike me. I was Finn Winchester. I had women tripping over themselves to get to me, but this woman, well she was special.

"I wouldn't say we've met yet, so I don't really know that you can say it's nice to meet me," She had a slight attitude and I suddenly felt alive again. This woman had no idea who I was. She wasn't flirting with me and trying to win me over because she wanted my fame or money. She literally had no clue and I loved it.

I couldn't stop myself from chuckling as her eyes ran over my body. Her eyes lingered slightly too long on my chest and I knew she was as attracted to me as I was to her. "I noticed you and your sister coming into the bar—"

"She's not my sister, she's my friend." She cut me off in a dismissive tone and I could tell she was trying to put me in my place. Only she had no idea who she was dealing with.

"You're both very beautiful." I took a sip of my beer. "But you seem particularly fiery." I liked fiery. Fiery meant passionate. Fiery meant she had an opinion. Fiery meant she wouldn't be my yes woman.

"Sorry, not tonight." I could see her face shutting down and I frowned. What had I done wrong?

"Not tonight what?" I raised an eyebrow. Was she a mindreader? Did she know I wanted to take her back to my apartment and fuck her brains out? Though I knew I couldn't even if I wanted to as my buddy, Brody was in town and staying with me until he got his own place. And tonight he'd planned a special meal for some broadway actress he'd met. Hence me being at that bar. "Can I not be a gentleman?"

"We both know what you want." She pressed her lips together and licked them quickly and all I wanted to do was kiss her.

"What I want?" I shook my head. Trust me honey, you have no idea what I want. "You're the one that asked me if I saw something I liked?"

"That wasn't an invitation into my bed."

"It doesn't have to be in a bed." I licked my lips slowly.

I'd fuck her anywhere. In a bed, the bathtub, on the couch, on my desk in my office. Shit, if she wanted me to, I'd fuck here right here at the bar; but something told me that was the furthest thing from her mind.

"I'm going to have to say not tonight, not ever, no thank you." She turned away from me and I knew she was done with our conversation. And that simple act let me know that this woman, whoever she was, was the one for me. She had spunk and attitude and holy hell, she was the most gorgeous woman I'd ever seen. Even though she'd turned away from me, I could still see the fire in her brown eyes. I stared at her as she stood there, tapping her foot in beat to the music and singing along to the ACDC song that was playing. And in that moment I knew as sure as I knew my own name, that I was going to marry her one day. I didn't know her name. I didn't know if she had a boyfriend. I didn't know anything other than what the words in my heart were saying. This one's special, Finn. This one will change your life.

Thank you for reading P.S. Never in A Million Years! I hope you enjoyed it. The next book in the series is P.S. Not if You Were The Last Man on Earth.

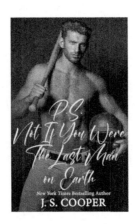

To my tent mate,

I am only going to say this once. I am not interested in you. I will not be sharing a sleeping bag with you. I will not be asking you to

keep me warm with your 'hot body'. Who calls their own body

hot by the way? I will not be doing a belly dance for you in the middle of the night and I definitely won't be making you hot chocolate. You'll be lucky if I even alert you to a bear, so don't push your luck. I'm going to be 100% honest with you. I'm not interested and have no desire to see you again after this trip.

Yours Unsincerely,

Susie

P.S. Not if you were the last man on earth

They say that no good deed goes unpunished and they are surely right.

I agreed to go on a camping trip with my best friend and her new boyfriend, Finn, but I never agreed to share a tent with Finn's best friend, Brody.

Brody is a pompous full of himself jock. He thinks he rules the world because he's some hot shot baseball player, but the jokes on him because I don't even watch sports. I just need to get past this weekend without killing him and then I never have to deal with his arrogant ass again.

ACKNOWLEDGMENTS

2022 started off with a bang. Not a year after burying, my great aunt passed away. I couldn't believe I had to plan a second funeral in less than a year. I knew that I wanted to write something fun and light to put me in the right mood finally, and for fun, I named some of the characters after my mum, great aunt and myself.

Marcia is named after my mum, Faye Marcia.

Susie is named after me, Jaimie Suzi.

Lilian is named after my great aunt, Lilian Enid.

And Shantal is just a random name, haha. :)

I thought it would be a fun way to include the three of us in a fun series, without being to on the face. I really hope you enjoy the series.

As always thanks to my beta readers for this book: Andrea Robinson, Penny Leidecker , Kim McDonnell, and Kelly Gunn. I am always appreciative of all your help!

To the members of my street team, you put a smile on my face every day! Thank you!

Here's to 2022 being everything we hope for and more!

Jaimie
XOXO

Printed in Great Britain
by Amazon

77547286R00139